Obrion turned and walked back in the direction he thought he had come from.

A bright red oval appeared in the section of wall. He reached out to touch it and his hand disappeared. He pulled it back and looked at it. There was nothing wrong.

Putting both arms out in front, he walked into the glowing oval—and stepped out into the curving passage. There was no one to his right or left. He turned around in time to see the portal fade away. He stepped up to the place where it had been and put out his hand. The doorway appeared again, and disappeared when he pulled his hand back.

As he stood there, he realized that no technology of his time could possibly have produced this kind of doorway. This entire place was a functioning relic from a past which could not possibly have existed. He felt a stirring of prideful resentment toward a past culture that could have built this entire structure. It was the kind of thing one might expect of humanity's future, a goal to work toward. If the past had achieved what he saw, then the present was a time of decline. How would the world receive such evidence of its lesser status?

But Obrion knew the world would never know . . . he would never escape from this polar prison.

LASER BOOKS now available wherever books are sold!

For more information see the back pages of this book.

GEORGE ZEBROWSKI

THE STAR WEB

Cover
Illustration by
**KELLY
FREAS**

Laser **Books**

Toronto • New York • London

For Dan Galouye, who helped when
help was most needed ... at the beginning

THE STAR WEB

A LASER BOOK/first published 1975

ISBN 0-373-72015-7

Printed in U.S.A.

1. A Voice From The Cold

Something had come to life beneath the Antarctic ice, something that was bleeding patterned but unrecognizable radio signals, pulsing strongly enough to be reported by the earthwatch station in polar orbit, whispering from the edge of the world, from a place where there should have been only silence.

Standing on the white surface under a clear blue sky, Juan Obrion imagined a presence buried deeply beneath his heavy boots. Around him the packed ice and snow filled the Antarctic valley like ice cream in a rocky bowl, leaving only the mountainous rim to sight.

What was it? How deep, he wondered. A few hundred feet, a mile? The mountains were almost three miles high. How large a device was it? It did not seem to be a natural phenomena. What was its power source? How long had it been here, and what had moved it to speak?

He turned and walked back to the snowcab where the rest of the investigation team was unpacking the electronic gear that would help pinpoint the source of the strange signals.

The group included Lena Dravic, a Soviet-Norwegian paleontologist, Magnus Rassmussen, UN electronic inspections expert, Malachi Moede from Kenya, mechanic, tractor operator, amateur astronomer-jack-of-all-trades and military mercenary who had given up UN trouble shooting to help in the adventure of developing earth's own alien environment, Antarctica. Juan Obrion was an exobiologist who had turned polar expeditions director.

A week ago Titus Summet, coordinator of UN Earth Resources Security, had ordered them to search out this thing regardless of delay to other work. Juan knew that the others were as impatient as he to get to the end of the matter and return to their own projects before the Antarctic summer came to an end. He could feel their resentment at having to be here; it was the same as his own.

Yet there was something strange about this place, something inevitable in the presence of such a mysterious phenomena in the icebound Antarctic valley. For a moment it amused him to watch the way his mind conjured up uncritical suspicions independently of his approval. A scrap of information, an irrational image, even a fond wish that something could be true—all this went into the mix that supported the emergence of a variety of judgements and conclusions. And if a sudden fact appeared to support any kind of structure, simple or elaborate, it would have the effect of a spark in a volatile mixture; he would rush toward the implications.

The entire situation here was beginning to look like his kind of problem, and he found himself enjoying it. He valued the intellectual and emotional perception of the unknown, knowing that together with the catalyst of curiosity the process released the play of human creativity. Mind and knowledge are finite, while what can be known seems endless, and what can be imagined is endless. The intensity of enjoyment made life worth living, he thought, while the unknown holds us in suspense between suspicion and discovery . . .

He walked up to the tractor cab, threw back the hood of his parka and climbed inside where Malachi Moede was listening to the radio wail of whatever was embedded in the ice.

"Why aren't you helping outside, Mal?"

The black Kenyan smiled at him, showing teeth like milk in an inkwell. "Magnus doesn't trust anyone with his gear except Lena, claims she's more careful, the old chauvinist bounder."

The radio sound silenced them for a moment. It reminded Juan of a perfectly formed carrier signal, an alarm repeating endlessly, devoid of all except prearranged information.

"Why did they send you?" Malachi asked. "And why me? Why duplicate abilities? What does Summet know that he hasn't told us?"

"Somebody got Titus all worked up about the importance of this thing—probably a military—enough for him to send out two hounds. Makes him feel better. But you and I are different, we know a lot of other things too."

Through the forward windshield they could see Magnus Rassmussen and Lena Dravic pulling the small radar sled across the ice. The sled gained speed but they stopped it at a previously set thousand yard red flag marker.

"There are only a few explanations about this," Juan said, "and I can throw most of them away."

Malachi sighed. "Back at Oxford during my childhood there was a feeling that the universe had all been collected, by Queen Victoria actually, and we were not to show surprise at anything startling—as if we could look it up for ourselves in the place where they store extraordinary things. I wonder what the increase in knowledge has done to them. Ignorance is probably good manners now." He paused. "Tell me what you think is going on here."

Juan shrugged. "You guess first."

"After you—you're ready with at least one or two thoughts, maybe they'll suggest something to me."

"Okay, one it's something natural we've never encountered before. Two, it's something belonging to a UN member. Three, it's extraterrestrial. Four, it's from the past."

"That's it?"

"All I've got, Mal."

Rassmussen and Lena Dravic looked like lumpy bears coming back across the ice. Juan stared at them as he listened to Malachi's answer.

"Your first idea reminds me of the flap thirty years ago about signals from intelligent life out in the galaxy, and that turned out to be a rotating neutron star—a pulsar—emitting signals like a lighthouse. Completely natural but it seemed very intentional at the time—but that was the only time. I don't think this belongs to a UN member, or anybody else—"

"They told you more than they told me, I see."

"I was to tell you. That leaves your last two guesses. When you say something from the past, I take it you mean an advanced civilization?"

"It would have to be."

"The extraterrestrial theory is always an open one, I suppose . . ."

"Or your information is bad and it does belong to a UN member. It wouldn't be the first time someone has lied to the UN."

Lena opened the cab door next to Juan and

shouted, "Shall we finish setting up the camp quarters now? We don't have all year."

"We'd better, Juan," Malachi said as he opened the door on his side. "It's better to work in the dear old sunlight."

AT NIGHT the frozen continent seemed to receive its chill from the endless icy stars wheeling about the south pole. The insulated hut was a black shadow standing on a blue-white plain. The mountains were black teeth on the horizon. Four human figures emerged and stood looking up at the sky . . .

"There it is," Juan Obrion said, pointing.

From behind the molar-like mountains a bright star rose, Polar Earth Station One, climbing slowly toward the zenith.

Obrion led the way to the snowcab. He opened the door and climbed inside. Malachi and Rassmussen climbed in next to him in the front seat. Lena pulled herself into the back seat in one fluid motion. Malachi slammed the door shut and sat back heavily. Rassmussen's tall thin frame seemed hunched over the glowing instrument panel.

Juan waited for the second hand of the clock to reach the appointed moment and opened the channel to the station in the sky. Rassmussen pushed the button which activated the radar substation he and Lena had set up earlier.

Malachi made voice contact. "Signals very clear. What are your coordinates for the location of the source?"

Lena had turned on a light over the rolling map drum in the back seat.

An impersonal voice from the orbital station began to read off co-ordinates.

When it was finished Lena said, "But that's here, all around us. How large can this thing be?"

"Triangulation with your substation is accurate," Earthwatch One said, "your source must lie in the circle where you are the center and the radius extends to the substation, perhaps beyond . . . we are also picking up mascon readings from this area. The material below you is exceptionally dense compared to the surroundings."

Juan opened the channel to the mysterious signal. Suddenly the perfectly symmetrical wail seemed like a crying in a huge empty auditorium where the house lights were stars. The sound was set in a great silence, a solitude that suggested an opened vastness, a space of feeling and pride beyond anything Juan had ever known . . . .

There was nothing left to do now except make preparations to excavate.

IN THE MORNING the big copters appeared with the heavy digging machinery. Juan Obrion watched them as they beat across the blue from the north like giant insects and set down one by one within the circle of red flags which now outlined the area of ignorance. Summet had promised fifteen machines, with all the equipment and supplies necessary to the task, together with a hundred men to do the heavy labor. He had been true to his word.

By noon one heavy steel rotary digger had gone down a hundred feet to shatter itself against a hard surface of some kind; by one o'clock the same thing had happened in a spot two hundred feet away. Two big scoops were brought into place and they began to dig a large hole between the two smaller holes made by the rotaries. Fifty feet down the scoops ran out of reach, forcing the workers to stop. The rest of the day was spent in widening the hole and constructing a forty five degree ramp of packed snow down into the crater for one of the smaller scoops to use.

As it grew dark, Juan and Malachi watched the excavators set up huge floodlights around the site, along with the portable generators which picked up their daily power load through the microwave transmissions from orbital solar plants. The compact batteries could store up to seventy-two hours of electrical power, more than enough to last until the next feed from orbit. One by one the microwave dishes were lined up to catch the power station as it came up over the horizon, and each ear would sweep one hundred eighty degrees until the source was lost to sight at the other edge of the world. Against the darkening blue of the sky, the ears were black circles, expectant sentries listening inside a hollow universe . . .

Juan watched as the small scoop rolled down into the crater to eat away at the hard ice at the bottom. The ice began to look dark in the harsh glare of the blue-white plasma lamps.

The crews were working in shifts around the clock, under strict orders. Lena and Rassmussen had long ago gone to sleep. Juan and Malachi had come out twice during the night.

"The color of that ice," Malachi said, "it's not just the lights."

"It bothered me too," Juan said.

Suddenly there was a grinding sound and the

scoop was quiet. Juan moved to his left at the edge to get a better view.

At the bottom of the crater a section of something black protruded from the ice like a portion of some huge swimming beast trapped below, no longer capable of motion through whatever sea had first contained it.

Juan walked past Malachi and down the ramp. Malachi followed. The workers had stepped back from what they had uncovered. The claw of the scoop was frozen in mid air. The operator had climbed out onto the tread and was staring at what he had found.

Juan came up to the thing and squatted down to feel the surface with his gloved hand. He made a fist and struck it. One of the diggers came up to him and handed him a small geologist's hammer. Juan struck once lightly. The only sound was a dull metallic thud. In a wild moment he had almost expected the beast to move and shake the ice. . .

"We're going to try going through this," Malachi said kneeling down next to him. "I don't think this belongs to anyone we know, old man."

"How big do you think it is?"

"No way to tell, yet. The first dig holes are two hundred feet apart and this is in the middle. We could drill more holes and widen them out like this one."

"You pick the spot and give the orders," Juan said. "Then we had better get some sleep. Lena and Magnus will wake us if anything new happens."

Juan stood up and led the way out of the crater. There was a faint hint of dawn light coming up from behind the mountains. For a moment he wondered what he was doing here, what this crazy digging was all about, and what were all these unlikely theories he and Malachi had started coming up with. He staggered toward the hut thinking of sleep.

LENA WAS SHAKING him awake, gently.

"Juan, there's an opening, wake up."

He opened his eyes and saw the high cheekbones and blue eyes of her face hovering over him. Behind her Malachi was sitting in a chair drinking coffee. The white coffee cup seemed to match his teeth, and for a moment before his vision cleared Juan thought it was a huge tooth. Through the small window in the direction of his feet he could see it was evening again. Suddenly he resented Antarctica. Where were the sunny beaches and the simple pleasures he had not known for so long? Where was the love affair he had put off for so long now? What was this thing under the ice which was quickly becoming a nagging puzzle? He imagined a city standing on the soil of a continent locked in ice. Whatever it turned out to be, he knew he would resent it.

Slowly he got up and slipped into his insulated coverall which went on over the thermal indoor suits they all wore. "What do you mean, Lena?" he asked as Malachi gave him a cup of coffee.

"We've found an opening into the thing," Malachi said, "she only repeated it nine times."

Obrion started pacing next to his bunk while sipping his coffee. "I expected that there would be one." He put the cup on a chair. "Let's get out there."

BLUE LIGHT was streaming upward from the crater. As Juan followed Malachi down into the new opening, the light radiated upward as if cast by a blue sun below the horizon.

Magnus Rassmussen was standing over a circular opening, his profile thrown into a strange shadow cast upward by the blue glare. Juan came up to the well of light and stood looking down as if into an oceanic eye. Lena and Malachi walked around to his left and stared down silently.

"Mal, you come with me," Obrion said.

Lena and Rassmussen did not protest as Juan sat down on the edge of the opening and let his feet hang down inside. The blue seemed warm and he felt as if he were entering the waters of an exotic bath. His feet brushed against a wall and found ladder-like ridges. He turned and lowered himself on his gloved hands until he could grasp one of the ridges with his left hand.

"It's only five feet to the bottom," Lena said. "We dropped a line before."

Rassmussen dropped the line again as she spoke. "It's there if you need it, Juan," the engineer said.

Juan reached out for the next ridge with his boot. Suddenly his foot slipped. He grasped the line and slid down quickly. Looking up immediately he saw Malachi coming down after him. Lena and Magnus were dark figures above, giants in the lighted circle.

The footing was solid. In a moment Malachi was standing next to him. Obrion peered around the chamber, trying to guess its size.

"You go left," Obrion said, "I'll go right—but not too far."

"Juan!" Lena shouted from above. "The cover is closing—"

He looked up in time to see a glowing red circle. Then the opening was gone, with nothing to suggest that there had ever been one. Quickly he walked directly under the place where it had been. Mal came up and stood next to him.

The circle glowed and Juan was looking at Lena and Magnus again. "It's automatic," Lena said loudly. "The diggers said it appeared out of nowhere the first time also."

"I see now," Malachi said. "When there was no one inside here the opening was triggered by anyone who came near outside. But while we're inside, only we can open it. That's a safety feature of a lock system, it seems, completely automatic." He looked around. "There's got to be an inner entrance leading inside, so that we can clear the chamber for others to use from outside. But that probably won't open until the one above closes. The only way to find it is to make a circuit of the chamber."

"Do you think this could be a city?" Obrion asked. "Was it once under water—hence the lock?"

"We'll know more when we get inside," Malachi said as he started to feel his way around the room.

"I don't think there's anyone here," Juan said. He stepped to one side and the opening above faded away in a faint red glow. "We'll get trekking packs and take a look-see trip inside before someone puts a clamp on the whole find. It would be just like Titus to come down here himself and rob us. If we're good enough to leave our work to find this thing, then we should get the credit, don't you think?"

"Righto, Juan—do you realize what this means? Incredible, but there is a buried culture in Antarctica

. . . you don't suppose this could be a hoax, an elaborate plant made by some eccentric millionaire?"

"Suits me fine, whatever it is," Obrion said. "I'll get the others and we'll get to work."

"It couldn't be a hoax," Malachi added, "not with that kind of lock."

AS THEY STOOD to one side looking up at the circle of night through which they had entered, it glowed and disappeared.

"Hello, I've found it—the inner door!" Malachi shouted.

Obrion turned and saw an orange glow spilling out from the new circle. He walked forward and stepped through into a corridor which seemed covered with hard obsidian. Overhead, orange-yellow lamps curved away to the left. The black floor reflected the lights as a dull white streak.

The others stepped through behind him. Obrion waited until the portal had disappeared before leading the way forward. They would explore while the crew slept above them, exhausted from the digging. Obrion had gained eight to ten hours before the foreman called in a report, at best a day before Summet arrived with his baggage of worldly consequences and locust-like experts, including UN military security teams. He shuddered at what the security and military personnel would see in this thing. It was certain they would try to turn it to their advantage in terms of appropriations and practical authority.

Obrion loosened a shoulder strap on his backpack, threw back the hood of his parka and adjusted the position of the emergency light on his hooded cap. As he walked forward, he started to feel very protective about the structure, as if he had been its architect, almost as if it were enlisting his help, leading him on with promises of strange rewards, stirring his curiosity in a way he had not known since he had been a small boy . . .

"The curve of the corridor is a spiral leading down," Malachi said from behind. "My level indicates we're moving lower into this thing."

"Look at the markings on the walls," Lena said.

Obrion stopped. Immediately ahead was a large circular opening cut in the floor. The corridor continued on the other side. They walked up to it together and looked down.

The passage was filled with bright yellow light and went straight down as far as they could see. Warm air was coming up from it, air that seemed to be overly rich in oxygen. Obrion took a coin out of his pocket and dropped it in. The coin floated down slowly, as if something were holding it in a vise-like grip.

"Curious," Rassmussen said as he watched, "it stays flat, in the position it had when you let go."

"Heeeeeeeeeeeeeeeey!" The sound came from behind them in the corridor. They all turned suddenly. Next to Obrion, Malachi staggered back from the load of his pack and stepped into the opening in the floor.

"Juan, help me," he said desperately.

Obrion turned in time to see him moving downward. He fell to his knees at the edge, as did Lena and Magnus. They all reached down with their hands, but Malachi was too far down, falling slowly away, yet held aloft as if by some force, a man in an invisible elevator. Obrion could see him moving his lips as if in prayer, but all sound seemed cut off.

Gradually his figure dwindled to the size of a toy doll, then to a dark point, and in another instant Malachi Moede was gone.

"HEEEEEEEEEEEEEEEEEY!" The sound repeated itself behind them, as if to confirm with a banshee's glee the loss of Malachi, one of Africa's new men, newly swallowed by a mechanical leviathan hibernating in the land of cold.

"Heeeeeeeeeeeeeeeeey!"

Obrion, Lena and Rassmussen got up and turned to face whatever was coming down the curving corridor after them.

"It was louder," Lena said.

For a few moments Juan heard only their breathing, and even that grew quieter as they waited. The passage seemed to be filled with a blue mist.

Footsteps.

"Juan, what could it be?" Lena whispered.

Obrion shook his head, motioning her to be silent.

Rassmussen came up and stood at his left, readying himself. Obrion slipped off his pack and placed it at his feet. Rassmussen did the same. They had no weapons except their bare hands.

At the bend of the passage two figures appeared in silhouette, coming partially into view and stopping, two cutouts made of black paper, standing perfectly still . . .

Then Obrion noticed that they were growing larger, shadows coming forward to engulf them, threatening as if in a bad dream. This is the real world, he said to himself silently; but all the events here were fantastic. The structure he was in was fantastic, yet certainly real; its very reality seemed to promise that the store of the fantastically real was far from exhausted.

Slowly Obrion walked forward to meet the shadows.

2. The Seekers

The shadows seemed to retreat as he approached them.

"Juan!" Lena shouted with concern in her voice.

Suddenly the shadows dissolved into two human figures. The one on the right was tall, with blonde hair and blue eyes. He was stocky even for a man wearing a snowsuit. The man next to him was middle sized, with graying brown hair and a familiar set of bushy eyebrows, their brown wires still untouched by gray.

"Titus Summet!" Obrion shouted. "What are you doing here?" The anger rose up in him. "Do you realize what your intruding has just cost us—we've lost Malachi—"

"Ivan Dimitryk, this is Juan Obrion—"

"Titus, there's no time to stand and chat. You helped cause a serious accident."

"Where?" Juan saw the frightened smile on the UN Director's face.

"Come see."

He led them back to Lena and Rassmussen, and for a moment they all stared down into the drop.

"He must be dead," Summet said. "I don't see how anyone could survive a fall like that. Let's get out of here. We'll be setting up a large base dome before getting into this thing any more." Suddenly Juan hated the older man's cold British tones, his lack of concern for Malachi's life, as well as the rude hint that he was about to assume command.

"We don't think he's dead, Titus," Juan said.

"Oh, why?"

"Well, you see, he didn't exactly fall. It seemed more like he floated down. He's in another section of this thing and we've got to find him."

"What do you think, Rassmussen?" Summet asked.

"I tend to agree with Juan."

"Very well, we shall come back when we're better equipped for a search."

Juan was still angry as he led the way out.

SUMMET HAD INSISTED on the weapons. Obrion did not like wearing a gun, and he could tell that Lena tolerated her own as she would a jawbone club attached to her waist. They had brought additional provisions and first-aid supplies to add to their backpacks which they had left near the drop tube.

At the drop, Obrion led the way around, followed by Lena, Summet, Rassmussen and Ivan Dimitryk. Ahead the passage continued in a slow curve, leading downward like a spiralling wormhole cutting through an apple. Juan played with the image suggested by the corridor: a solid sphere locked in the ageless ice. The impression seemed very immediate, almost as if it had been placed into his mind. *Malachi, you can't be dead,* the thought intruded. He could not accept the picture of his friend's body lying broken at the bottom of the strange well. Then he realized that there should be doors in a corridor, unless the passage was for some kind of vehicle.

"Juan," Lena said behind him as they walked, "there's a sound coming from ahead, can't you hear it?"

He stopped and listened. Gradually a high whine became audible enough to be more than suggestion.

"I can hear it," Summet said. Juan detected a note of fear in his voice, while in his own mind grew the image of a snakelike vehicle pushing through the curving passage to crush them.

"Quick, everyone against the wall!" Obrion shouted.

They all took a few steps to their right and waited with backs to the wall. As he started to lean against the surface, Obrion felt it yield and he stumbled backward under the weight of his pack—

—and found himself in a brightly lit room, alone.

THE SILENCE WAS oppressive. The harsh white light made the skin of his hands seem almost transparent. Around him were benches of various sizes, and standing things that looked like cabinets. Juan sat down to catch his breath. He heard his heart beating loudly in his chest. He heard his pulse in his ears . . . distant plodding footsteps.

Suddenly the ceiling turned a dull red and he felt heat penetrate to every part of his body. He started to sweat in his heavy clothing. Then the ceiling changed back to white and he felt a cool breeze rush through the room. There was a sweet scent in the air, pleasant yet similar to the sweetness of pure oxygen.

He turned and walked back in the direction he thought he had come from. A bright red oval appeared in the section of wall. He reached out to touch it and his hand disappeared. He pulled it back and looked at it. There was nothing wrong. Putting both arms out in front, he walked into the glowing oval—and stepped out into the curving passage. There was no one to his right or left. He turned around in time to see the portal fade away. He stepped up to the place where it had been and put out his hand. The doorway appeared again, and disappeared when he pulled his hand back.

As he stood there, he realized that no technology of his time could possibly have produced this kind of doorway. This entire place was a functioning relic from a past which could not possibly have existed. He felt a stirring of prideful resentment toward the past culture that could have built this entire structure. It was the kind of thing one might expect of humanity's future, a goal to work toward. If the past had achieved what he saw, then the present was a time of decline. How would the world receive such evidence of its lesser status?

Back along the passage, the others began to appear as each in turn learned the mechanism of the doors. Most likely the entire length of the winding passage was spaced with entranceways, probably on both sides. For a moment the room he had left reminded him of a bath.

There was a look of personal pride on Summet's face. "Juan, we're going no further—these rooms come first. We have got to start taking photographs. I've just seen some very curious things. What happened to you?"

"I think I just took a bath . . . I'm not sure. Titus, all this, it doesn't disturb you?"

"Not very much, really. Why should it? It's the

archeological find of the century. Whatever it is, we'll figure it out."

"What do you think it is, Titus?" Rassmussen asked from behind him.

The director turned around to face Magnus, then turned back to Obrion. "You're all trying to needle me. I warn you . . ." Then he smiled. "Why not, I try to be in a good mood."

"Well, what do you think this is?" Lena asked.

The worldly man shrugged his wide shoulders, wrinkled his bushy brown eyebrows and said, "For one thing, it's an Earth Resource as of right now, and fully protected by my . . . by the authority of UN Resources Security. Everyone will get his share—nations, scientists, everyone, depending on why they need it and what good it will do. For now, everyone out back topside! That's an official order."

Juan looked at Ivan Dimitryk, who stood next to the director. There was a satisfied look on his face.

Lena sighed. "You're forgetting we have to look for Malachi."

"I'll take the responsibility, Dravic. Now move, or I'll go get some security police." He started to herd them before him, preferring to bring up the rear with Dimitryk. "We'll all search better after we get some sleep. Oh, leave your packs near the entrance. No sense carting them around."

"Shut up, Titus," Obrion said. "You can order us about, but we're still bright enough to think of little things for ourselves."

In the quiet Juan remembered how Malachi had openly mocked the director, in cutting ways that would always be superior to the angry kick in the pants Titus deserved.

As he lay in his bunk, Juan wondered about what they were getting into. Summet had become very nervous by the time they had gotten back to quarters, as if he were afraid that some disaster would rob him of his prize. Obrion's own work seemed a distant thought next to Malachi's absence and the thought of exploring the buried structure. There would be years of work here . . .

He should have insisted that the search for Malachi go forward immediately, but they were all tired and needed what sleep was left in the remaining night hours. He fell asleep dreaming of sea birds crying loudly under a burning sun . . .

BEHIND THE PARTITION in her corner of the cabin, Lena was warm under the electric blanket. Malachi was wheeling away from her into the bowels of a nameless construction and she remembered the feeling of helplessness which was a cold whirlwind passing through all of them. Yet she felt reasonably sure that Malachi had not fallen to his death. She could not imagine the strong African dead.

Summet was a meddler. Juan had told her of his troubles with the director. The man had to be emotionally blackmailed to get things done. Facts counted only as convincers. Summet depended on those around him for advice, and often got the best through a process of elimination and delay; but a thing still had to look good politically to be implemented. The director was a device brought into being by circumstances involving science and world affairs. Politicos trusted him and world science knew that he could be convinced by their best spokesmen. She tried to imagine Titus Summet as the environmental biologist he had been trained to be, and failed.

Summet depended on Juan's combination of skills. There were not many exobiologists who had his organizational abilities and high standing in the scientific community. In Summet's position of power Juan would have been envied. A tall, black-haired aristocrat from a Spanish-American California family, Juan could easily charm a public gathering with his fluid bodily movements and noble posture. Summet was a master at looking naturally uncomfortable and trustworthy at the same time, especially to people who were planning to spend money. She could not remember him ever appearing with Juan in public.

She wondered why Ivan Dimitryk was here. There was something about his presence that suggested a Soviet protest, or at least a move to steal some glory for Russian science. The official status of such interlopers was "UN Observer." Summet had been obliged to bring one along, a sign of his servile position to the world above his authority. It was obvious that Dimitryk was contemptuous of the director. She smiled to herself at the Russian's ridiculous image, one which reminded her of Texans touring Europe. She was beginning to feel some sympathy for Titus as she fell asleep.

MAGNUS RASSMUSSEN knew enough about energy conversions to realize that the dissolving doorways inside the structure involved a manipulation of power on a level of sophistication unknown in his experience, or the experience of any engineer in recorded history, if the record of the past was to be believed.

Such a control of the fluid aspects of matter-energy was a dream. Its reality implied a revolution in the world's economic system through the capability for the synthesis of any scarce items from any kind of raw material. And here the application was used to operate doors! There had to be other applications elsewhere in the structure.

He felt lucky to be here. Raising his head, he looked around in the dark at the sleeping bodies in the cabin. Through the small window the sky was already light blue with dawn. He thought of the radio beacon marking a new world below the ice. Where was Malachi now, he wondered. What strange things was he seeing?

The question was like a solid object in his brain as he fell asleep.

HANDS REACHED OUT to Malachi as he fell, hands which seemed to grow longer with the downward effort. He saw the look of horror in the faces of his friends as the world opened to swallow him. Their expressions added to his terror, despite the sensation that he was sinking into quicksand rather than falling. He shouted, but gradually the circle of the opening above him grew smaller and disappeared. And suddenly he seemed to be moving faster. At any moment the bottom would rush up to meet him. His head would crack against a hard surface, snapping his spine . . .

Malachi screamed.

And a sadness took hold of him like the iron fist of some mad puppeteer jamming itself into the glove of the mannequin. He moved his arms wildly. But behind the crisis he remembered his grandmother telling him a story from a park bench. It was a story about a boy who fell into a bottomless well and reached a large ocean under the earth, where he learned to sail a pirate vessel, taking it to all the ports of the strange ocean where there was no sky or stars, only the glow of things which flew high in the caverns. The boy grew old in his new life, until a giant dropped a bucket into the well and fished him up ship and all . . .

Suddenly Malachi alighted on a small platform jutting out from the side of the drop tunnel. He stood shaking, surprised and frightened, but grateful for the reprieve. He noticed the small alcove which seemed to lead back into the complex. As he stepped into it, the wall dissolved to let him through—

—into a large circular room. The floor sloped downward toward the middle as in an amphitheater; the only chairs seemed to be standing in the center where the stage would be. Above him the space of the room was enormous.

Slowly he started to walk down the slope. Looking more closely toward the center, he noticed what looked like consoles of some kind spaced around the chairs, as if planned for some kind of work. For a moment it seemed to him that he should be able to guess what all this was for. His excitement increased as he drew near, almost as if his entire life had been lived to bring him to this place at this moment.

JUAN DREAMED of a large red weather balloon carrying him across the face of Antarctica. Lena was with him in the open basket, unafraid of the cold wind rushing by them. It seemed that the dream had been going on for ages when someone shook him gently awake. He opened his eyes, ready to push the intruder away.

Malachi was grinning at him, and motioning for him to be silent. "Get dressed," he whispered, "wake the others, except for Summet and his tag-along, and meet me at the entrance to the find." He got up from his kneeling position and turned to go, opening the inner door to the hut as Obrion was putting on his overpants. In a moment the outer door closed gently.

Juan felt the sudden absence of the anxiety which had been eating away at the back of his consciousness from the first minutes after Malachi's accident. He had restrained it, as they all had, together with their distaste for Summet.

When he was dressed he woke Lena, then Magnus. In fifteen minutes they were standing outside in the morning sun, squinting at him.

"Malachi's alive," he said, "he was just here and he wants us to meet him at the entrance to the structure, minus Summet and his friend."

"I'm so glad he's alive," Lena said.

Magnus sighed, obviously relieved.

Shivering in his parka, Obrion led the way past the cabins housing the excavation teams, past the helicopters squatting on the snow covered ice, toward the crater they had scooped out to placate human curiosity.

The weather was perfect again—a blue, cloudless sky, making for long, clear morning shadows. Obrion led them single file down into the crater.

Malachi was waiting at the entrance. Obrion grasped him by the hand; Lena hugged him while Magnus patted him on the back.

"I guess it wasn't my time," Malachi said, "much too early, really."

"How are you, what happened?" Lena asked.

"I'll have to show you." He turned and sat down on the edge of the circular entrance. "Follow me," he said and jumped down into the well of blue light.

One by one they followed him down into the opening. Once below, Juan reminded them all to put on the packs they had left for the next day's exploring. Finally they went after Malachi into the curving passageway. When they came again to the well, Malachi turned around and grinned. "Later we might all become adept at using this thing, but for now we'll have to hike the way I came out."

Obrion led the way after him down the continuing curve, thinking of all the hundreds of chambers hiding behind the sealed membranes of potentially fluid matter of which the doorways were made.

After a good quarter hour of marching, Obrion called after Malachi. "How much more?"

"Three or four kilometers," the black man said without turning around. "This is the long way."

For a moment Juan was surprised at his own easy acceptance of what they were doing, and the least of it was the fact that they were in technical violation of Summet's orders. But more importantly he realized that they knew nothing of what they were walking into. Their brains and senses drew a blank in terms of an explanation of what they were seeing. Only Malachi seemed to know something, and Malachi was a friend who had come back from near death as if in answer to a desperate wish.

"How big *is* this place?" Juan asked loudly.

In the amphitheater Obrion noticed that there were just enough fixed chairs for them all to sit down.

Malachi asked them to sit down before he spoke.

"Now watch this," he said. He sat down in the fourth chair. Now they were all facing each other. There was a rectangular console at each right hand. "You see I needed four people only."

"What are we supposed to see?" Lena asked.

"Now relax."

Rassmussen was drumming his fingers on the metallic surface of the seemingly blank solid growing out of the polished floor next to his chair.

Obrion found himself tensing.

"Sit back," Malachi was saying. "I had only a hint before. Wait."

Slowly, like the motion of a fine watch hand, the seats drew back, until they were all facing the space above the room. Obrion noticed that the light was everywhere, yet there was no direct source.

The circular chamber darkened quickly and he was looking at a starfield, intensely bright in the open darkness.

"All the brightest stars are G types," Malachi said, "single or double systems. The view seems to focus attention on them."

Suddenly the stars were gone. Obrion looked around in the dark, sensing that someone had stood up.

"Now look to your right," Malachi said.

The top of the rectangle next to Obrion had opened to reveal a complement of glowing controls. There was enough light from the four sets to reveal Malachi's dark shape standing nearby. Magnus was also up from his seat, peering closely at his own panel, his face a probing profile in the dim light. "What else have you found out?" Rassmussen asked.

"I have only one more thing to show," Malachi

said. "I have been thinking that this area here might be some kind of entertainment or educational center for the people who once lived here. We might as well face the idea that there was a high civilization in Antarctica well before recorded history. The date could be ten to fifty thousand years ago."

"There may be another explanation," Lena said, "but what we see is certainly real enough." The lights faded in as she spoke.

"Follow me," Malachi said.

He led the way out of the amphitheater, directly through the dissolving portal into the winding passage. Stepping across to the other side, Malachi activated another portal and stepped inside. Obrion followed, with Lena and Rassmussen right behind him, into a room which reminded him of the one he had visited before, except that this one was entirely bare.

A half dozen skeletons covered the floor, naked in the white light. Some were piled together, their bones mixed; others lay lonely near the corners.

"I've looked at them carefully," Malachi said. "They're not any human I've ever seen or heard about. There are dozens of minor differences, as well as some major ones. Two opposable thumbs on each hand and a very large ribcage. I would like to have seen the heart that once beat in one of these gentlemen. Their physical characteristics were natural evolutionary ones, or they were biologically engineered. Both notions are fantastic enough."

"What killed them?" Lena asked. "They seem to have died suddenly."

Obrion thought he felt the ground tremble slightly under his feet.

"That's probably a slippage in the ice around us," Malachi said. "This entire structure might no longer be resting on the bedrock of the continent. The glaciers might have sheared it off when they covered everything. It might not be safe."

There was another, smaller tremor, then quiet. Obrion listened for the vibrations but they did not return. "You know," he said looking around at the remains, "if they were like us, basically, then we can find out all about them. There will be points of subjective as well as external analogy. Psychologically there will already be a bridge between ourselves and them. They shared the same planet with us when we were ape folk struggling to differentiate ourselves from the other simians . . ."

"Perhaps," Malachi said, "but only if we can run our minds forward to at least grasp the look, the qualities of the kind of technics we might have a thousand years from now. Magnus, what do you think?"

Rassmussen shook his head. His tall, gray-haired frame seemed frail in the antiseptic light. "A hundred years might well give us some of the things I've seen here. Predictions are always conservative because the hard-to-imagine kinds of things seem remote and strange. But that can be deceptive. We're not used to it—it's not part of daily experience. Later it may seem simple and easy to accomplish. Any sufficiently advanced technology will look like magic, if you're backward enough . . ."

"But all of this is not magic," Malachi said. "You can *imagine* how it works, Magnus?"

"I think so, though it would be a long time before I could learn enough to do it all myself, without coaching. Instrumental skill is a different thing from being able to furnish an explanation. A technician can create an effect without having an adequate theory. In fact he may even be able to do things on the basis of a wrong theory. It doesn't follow that just because something *works* the theory is true; it may work for other reasons and the theory should be regarded as only possibly true. However, if something doesn't work, and all the conditions have been checked, then very likely the theory is false. Material things often seem to resist theory in practice, even when you feel certain that something must work. It took years to send and receive the first radio signals across the ocean. It was difficult to send a signal from one radio set to another sucessfully, across a room, even once."

"Everything in this place," Obrion said, "seems to have been working for a long time, possibly thousands of years. There's air, light, heat, living spaces. I'll bet there are adequately preserved stores of food somewhere. And maybe, Magnus, there is something in this place that might coax you into working miracles."

They all laughed. Juan looked at the skull on one of the skeletons, wondering what kind of smile it might have worn once.

"If I could even learn to make one of these doorways," Magnus said, "then I could solve the world's problems, the material ones at any rate."

Without warning the world trembled again, throwing them to the floor among the ancient bones, like marionettes whose strings had just been cut.

3. Trapped

The shaking and trembling continued, as if some percussive tunesmith were trying to throw the skeletons on the floor into a mad dance. Lena helped Obrion to his feet. Malachi did the same for Rassmussen. They passed through the dissolving portal in pairs and made their way up the curving incline of the passageway back to the entrance locks.

When they entered the outer lock-chamber forty minutes later, the shaking had stopped. The outer door dissolved overhead and they saw that the exit was completely blocked.

"Maybe it's not too thick a cover," Obrion said. "Boost me up, Mal."

When he was sitting up on Malachi's shoulders, Obrion started to dig with his hands. But the ice was hard and cold, and after a few minutes Malachi let him down. "We'll bloody our hands, even if we rotate," the Kenyan said, "and then we won't be able to do anything with our hands. We'll wait for Summet to dig us out."

"I hope he's angry enough to do it quickly," Obrion said.

"Let's hope he can guess where we are," Lena said.

"I suggest we make use of our time," Magnus said. "It will take a fair amount of time for them to dig through to us. In the meantime each of us could explore a room along the passageway. It's something useful we could do while we wait."

"If they take too long," Lena said, "we'll have to plan our survival, see about food and water in this place."

Obrion looked at his watch. "It's just past 9:00 a.m. If by this evening they haven't gotten us out, we'll go back to the circular room, take an inventory of what we left in our packs and start rationing while we search."

They were all silent for a few moments.

"Well, let's get started," Malachi said. Abruptly he turned and went through the portal back into the curving passage.

Lena and Rassmussen followed. Obrion brought up the rear.

FAR AHEAD OF Obrion, just before the turn in the passage, the small figure of Malachi went through the wall portal into a room. A minute before, Lena and Rassmussen had disappeared a hundred feet ahead of him. Obrion paused before doing the same. He was alone. The others had been swallowed up by the enigmatic chambers of the giant shell-like structure. It was as if they had all disappeared to avoid seeing the look of doubt in each other's eyes about the danger they were in. There was security in carrying out an assigned task, a sense of the normal.

Taking a deep breath, Juan pushed through the suddenly appearing red oval—

—into darkness.

As his eyes began to adjust, a scattering of small lights went on like distant stars overhead. He saw that he was in what seemed like a huge crypt. Human size caskets grew from the floor at even intervals, forming broken wheel spokes which led to a circular console in the center a hundred feet ahead. He walked up to it and turned to look around. The caskets, if he could call them that, were completely opaque and pale green. For a moment he imagined that he had walked into a surprise birthday party and at any moment hundreds of merry makers would rise up out of the coffins to cheer his health.

But the moment passed and the hall was quiet. He thought again about what was happening to them, how suddenly they had all been joined to these circumstances. Are we equal to discovering, even *guessing* what these things under the cold are for, he wondered; even if the guess were right, we would never know. Yet here was his chance—and a chance for all of them—to make their names.

He shivered in the seeming cold of the chamber despite his warm clothes.

As Lena passed through the sudden insubstantiality of the portal, fear blossomed inside her. What if somehow the portal were to freeze up around her as she went through? But before the terror of imagining her atoms mixing with the material of the wall could take hold, she was standing—

—in a completely bare room. There were no right angles. The walls curved like lenses looking out into fearful depths. It had to be an illusion; yet she felt there was something in the analogy. The room had been designed to be used exactly as she saw it. There was an infinity in its stillness, a perfection something like the sound inside a seashell, carrying from afar.

The light was indirect, softly white. She sat down on the smooth, perfectly clean floor and tried to put her thoughts in order. All of their scientific reputations were assured from this find, yet no one had mentioned it. She had not even thought of it, until now. One way or another, their lives would be changed. It would take years, perhaps lifetimes to explore, map and inventory the insides of the structure; even longer to understand what was here. Its very existence would alter human history as it had been written, changing it beyond recognition and in ways which would have seemed ridiculous if they had been put forward without overwhelming evidence, as imaginative creations.

But the floor she sat on was real, solid, or she was mad, hallucinating in some asylum and sharing the dream with Juan, Magnus and Malachi. No, these facts did not need to be invented. They needed to be understood.

Once again she felt the rush of curiosity coupled with the feeling that the room's visual evidence had already triggered a conclusion in her mind. It was the same feeling that the fascination of *explanation* in the sciences had produced in her as a girl; the same attraction she had felt upon learning why Norway had a midnight sun. To this day she associated inspiration and creativity with the midnight sun shining over snowy mountains. Knowledge was a glacier holding up the mountains. The slow accumulation of knowledge could save a life, or a world. It had done so many times, and would do so again. Whether for practical things, or for curiosity, her life would serve in this motion toward the light.

She looked around the room, realizing that she could not tell how large it was. Slowly she stood up and was perfectly still, imagining that if she could say the right words the walls would carry her sounds into the spaces between the stars.

MALACHI LOOKED AROUND at the various shapes growing from the floor like mushrooms. They seemed to be containers, hundreds of them covering the floor of the rectangular orange room. On both sides of him were shelves holding smaller box-like objects. The wall at the far end of the room was bare.

He was beginning to feel slightly deficient, and annoyed. Too much of what they had seen seemed to exist just beyond their immediate understanding. He walked up to two drums and tried to remove their covers. They would not move. He noticed a whole battery of the same kind against the right wall. He walked up to one and tried the cover, again without success.

They knew I was coming, he thought, so they sealed the covers.

RASSMUSSEN WAS STARING at a huge wall covered with empty cubbyholes, reminding him of a sold-out food automat. The rest of the blue-lighted room held a concentric arrangement of what seemed to be round tables complete with chairs. They must be tables and chairs, Magnus said to himself. And if the builders were like us, then perhaps we could eat the same food, if there was any in an edible state.

He wondered how many rooms there might be along the descending spiral of the passageway. How deeply into Antarctica did the spiral go? He imagined a huge hollow corkscrew stuck into the ice by a whimsical giant, with everything inside made deliberately puzzling, perhaps meaningless. But he recalled the elegance of the dissolving doorways, a reminder that to find how they worked was itself a way into much more than just another room.

WHEN JUAN CAME out again into the winding passage, he heard Rassmussen shouting.

"Help! Someone help me!"

Quickly he ran up along the way toward the engineer's voice. As he drew nearer, Juan saw the older man's hand frantically trying to claw its way through the dissolving portal. In a moment Juan saw that only Magnus' hand and face were visible. The rest of him was frozen in the substance of the doorway.

Juan came within a few feet of the face and looked into its eyes. "Are you hurt?"

"No—just stuck. Don't come near me, it might be dangerous."

The substance around Magnus seemed almost smokey, something that a good gust of wind might blow away. Magnus' face was a motionless mask. Only the eyes betrayed his fear.

Lena came out of the wall up ahead, followed almost immediately by the apparently smaller figure of Malachi further away.

"Quick!" Juan shouted. "Magnus is trapped!"

In seconds Lena and Malachi were by his side, looking with horror at the wall which showed a face and a hand, the face looking like a newly hung portrait just beginning to accept its fate, the hand moving as much as possible to keep up circulation.

"What can we do?" Lena asked.

"Can that stuff sever his hand?" Malachi asked in a whisper.

"I don't know," Obrion said. He imagined Magnus trapped forever in the wall. Food would be brought to him while team after team of the world's youngest physicist-engineers studied the mystery of the portal's mechanism. Nurses would bathe Rassmussen's face and brush his teeth after his meals; he would discuss his plight with aspiring rescuers in seminar after seminar, a revered magician tragically set in stone. And through the years the puzzle of the doorway would elude all who came to decipher it. *And what if it is a problem we are incapable of ever understanding,* Juan thought.

"Juan," Lena said speaking softly next to him, "with so much of his body enclosed he won't last very long."

Malachi said, "This is the first evidence we've seen that things in here are old and malfunctioning."

"Do you feel pain?" Lena asked.

"No . . . but my circulation is being affected, I am sure now I can't feel my hand. Funny . . . when I came through before . . . I would put up one hand as if I didn't believe it would work, and this time it failed."

They were all silent for a few moments.

"You may not be able to free me," Magnus continued, "so we'll have to face that possibility . . . that I may be dead by the time Summet digs us out."

As if offering a comment, the world trembled again for a moment, then was still.

"We'll get you out," Lena said.

Juan imagined Magnus' skull set in the wall like an ivory ornament; the long fingers of the fleshless hand were a hat hook . . .

"Of course!" Malachi said suddenly. "How stupid of us not to think of it." Before Obrion could react, the Kenyan stepped toward the portal which held Rassmussen. The familiar reddening of the oval appeared around the engineer's face and hand. Malachi grasped the wrist with both hands and pulled the trapped man out as the portal dissolved. "I was hoping this side could still be triggered to open on approach," Malachi said.

Rassmussen was sweating heavily in his parka, and his breath came slowly as Malachi held him up. The look of relief was plain in his face as Lena rubbed his limp hands.

"Can you stand now?" Malachi asked.

Magnus nodded. "Unfortunately we may have to go into that room again. It might contain things we need, or might come to need if we don't get out soon."

Malachi shrugged. "So the door sticks a bit. It might not happen again."

"Let's hope," Lena said.

Obrion thought of all the explorers who had died on this continent of cold at the edge of the world. Looking at Lena and Malachi and the recovering Magnus, he knew that none of them had any special charms of protection, including himself. Even if one were to die, it would poison the rest of his life, it seemed. They were all safe for the moment, but how long would luck last?

The floor shook again, more strongly this time. They all threw out their hands to keep balance.

As TITUS SUMMET watched the diggers trying to uncover the entrance to the buried complex, the continent shook with a force that knocked him on his back at the edge of the man-made crater. Instantly he was grateful. He might have been knocked forward to roll down into the depression.

But as he tried to stand up, the trembling continued, growing more violent with every second. Crawling on his hands and knees, Summet saw that that diggers at the bottom were strewn on the white like black pick-up sticks, each man holding on in the hope that the shaking would stop. As he watched, the bottom of the crater began to rise. An anger rose up inside him, almost as if he had expected any such silly event to have at least had the courtesy to file a permit with his office first.

The bottom of the crater and sides began to crack as they were pushed upward. Some of the diggers began to yell loudly for help. Summet stood up precariously and began to stagger back toward the huts and copters. Everyone was outside looking past him to the rising excavation site. He stopped and turned around. The crater's bottom was now at the level of his knees. At the highest point some ice had fallen away to show something dark pushing through. The diggers rolled downhill as the dome-like object pushed upward into view.

The ice cracks around it grew longer. He looked a few feet to his right and saw one pass him by, moving quickly toward one of the huts. With a numbed realization he guessed that whatever was pushing up was very large, large enough to push upward high enough so that their whole base, huts, digging machinery and helicopters, would be rolling downhill from the center. How could this be happening, he thought suddenly.

Dimitryk rushed up to him and tried to hurry him

along. "What could it be?" Summet asked as they started running. Dimitryk ran next to him, motioning at him to keep up the pace. Ahead of them, scores of men were fleeing like black penguins, trying to reach the copters.

As he ran, Summet tried to keep his self control. Deep down inside him he felt the impulse to scream, but he recognized it as a sign of possible shock. He looked right and left and saw that the cracks were all around them and radiating ahead like huge arteries from the crater. He felt the ice tilt upward behind him.

When they reached the command copter, Summet turned to see a giant dome growing up from the snowfield, rising like a huge brown bubble. Most of the work crews were in their copters. As the blades turned over above him, he hesitated, appalled at the size of the thing that had come so suddenly into his life. And Obrion, Rassmussen, Lena and Moede were inside. For a moment he felt a spasm of fear, then anger . . .

Someone grabbed him by the collar of his parka and pulled him inside the copter just as it was leaving the ground. Summet saw his own shadow and that of the whirly running across the crowding cracks.

"Are you well?" Dimitryk asked as he let go of Summet inside the open doorway. Summet looked out as the copter circled the titanic dome below.

"Yes, I'm fine—sorry old man," Titus said without looking at him.

The copters circled once, and again, like whaling boats waiting for the leviathan to disgorge those it had swallowed.

But for the moment all was still, as if the cold of Antarctica had quick-frozen all motion, except for the copters which refused to stick to the sky.

"I suspect," Summet said, "from the curvature we can see, that the dome might easily take up a quarter of the valley when fully exposed, don't you think?"

The Russian nodded. The wind coming past the open loading entrance whipped their visible breath away like spun glass.

"If it stays quiet," Summet said, "we'll land and try to pick up Obrion and his team. They should be able to get out now that the entranceway is no longer covered. The slope of the dome is still shallow enough to slide down, and—"

"They may be dead," Dimitryk said.

Summet looked directly at him, but the Russian continued staring out at the dome. "No reason to think that," Summet said. "They're just a bit blocked up, that's all. It's just a small quake pushing up some very old stuff. There's nothing there that could kill them. We're all safe and the quake is over. How old do you think it is?"

"There is no way to tell," the Russian shrugged, and was silent.

The Russian had been contemptuous of him from the first, and was more so now after seeing him blunder around in the out-of-doors. Titus had to admit to being out of shape, better suited to UN chambers and effective office procedures. He should not have come here, he thought glumly. Then he remembered the mini-camera in the elbow zip pocket of his parka. Reaching around, he brought it out with his left hand and began to snap color holos of the scene below. Hopefully, satellite cameras were also hard at work from above, and in a fuller range than just the visible spectrum.

"Give the order to land a ways off," Summet said

as he put the camera back in his pocket and zipped it up. "We've got to give Obrion's people some time. We don't want them coming out to find us gone. Oh, and radio for relief craft to come and take over our watch. Even if we have to send all these copters back, I want one or two crews here at all times. If everything stays put while we're still here, we'll walk up to the bloody thing and try to get inside. But we've got to play it carefully . . ."

Without a word of comment or the slightest sign of approval, the Russian stood up and made his way up to the pilot to relay the order. Summet looked after him into the passenger cabin, where more than a dozen men from the digging crews were crowding around the seat windows to see the strange object on the continent below. Summet began to feel foolish as he waited for Dimitryk to come back.

The Russian came back in two minutes, just as the first of the eight circling whirlies landed on the far side of the brown dome. The others dropped in low to form a half circle to the west of the cracks, landing one by one more than half a mile from the longest fissure. Dimitryk handed Summet one of the two pairs of binoculars he had brought back just as their copter landed.

Summet put the glasses up to his eyes and the round mountain was thrown up-close suddenly, breaking the foreshortened distance to the jagged peaks behind it. He scanned the surface, looking for a sign of the entrance. He tried to hold the lenses steady as he stood up in the entranceway, but a slight jiggling crept into the blue-framed visual field. The trembling increased, magnified by the power of the glass. Now he was sure that his hands were not shaking enough to cause the motion all by themselves.

Turning to Dimitryk he asked, "Do you see that tremble?"

The Russian nodded without lowering his binoculars.

Summet felt the nervousness in his stomach increase suddenly. "Let's get back in the air now. We can't trust what may happen, can we? And we may not get a chance to get off again properly. Can't risk all these lives, can we?" The ground began to tremble noticeably. Dimitryk lowered his glasses, grabbed a handhold and turned to shout something in Russian into the passenger cabin.

The trembling became violent just as the copter lifted. When they were high enough, Summet saw that the cracks were running again.

4. Icelock

The dome pushed upward.

Ragged chunks of ice fell in a rolling tumble down the increasing slope.

"We are running out of gas," Dimitryk said next to Summet. The Russian had put on his goggles, turning his eyes into twin mirrors reflecting the cloudless blue sky and an occasional flash of sunlight. "Summet, we cannot stay any longer. There will be no fuel."

"I know, I know—look!"

The dome had risen high enough now to buckle the slope around it into a vertical wall. A sound like thunder reached Summet's ears as large sections of the wall collapsed. The radiating fissures were now black crevasses, darkening arteries in the once unbroken white. Summet could not take his eyes away from the straining center of the thundering maelstrom.

"It must be at least two miles across," he said. "What can be pushing it up?" He had to shout to hear himself speak.

Suddenly there was a sharp sound, like a balloon bursting. The dome was a huge globe rising from the broken surface. Its skin was no longer brown. A pulsating silver glow enclosed the ball, an iridescent field seemingly pushing away the massive sections of ice still clinging to the sphere. In a moment the object was hovering level with the copters. As Summet watched, it jerked upward, suddenly pulling tons of ice after it from the surface, as if they were attached to invisible strings pulled tight abruptly. In seconds it was high above them, dwindling quickly into a black spot in the blue sky. The spot collapsed into a point and disappeared.

A roaring continued from below, where ice was collapsing into the titanic hole left by the globe. The sides which had been held apart for uncounted centuries gave way. The ice fell in like a niagara for more than five minutes, healing the wound in the continent.

"We can leave now," Summet said turning to Dimitryk, but the Russian had gone inside. He stood up, staggered into the passenger cabin and sat down next to Dimitryk. The men inside wore stunned looks on their faces, glancing only occasionally out the windows which circled the cabin behind their seats. The Russian was silent as Summet turned around to look out at the other copters following their lead away from the caved-in hole.

He felt defeated and drained. There was nothing to say. Summet thought of Obrion and his team, hurled suddenly through the sky.

Putting his face up close to the window, he strained to look back at the site, where a huge cloud of steam was belching upward toward the sun.

"DO YOU HEAR THAT?" Lena asked suddenly.

The shaking had stopped and everything seemed perfectly still.

"No, I don't," Obrion said.

"It's high frequency, I can barely pick it up myself."

"I wonder," Malachi said, "if it's a sound the builders of this place were supposed to hear. If it's a normal sound, then their hearing extended into a higher range."

"Good thing we have Lena to hear it for us," Rassmussen added. "It might be important."

"It seems to be coming from the room I was in before, Juan," she said and started to lead the way.

"Are you sure you're well?" Obrion asked Magnus as they followed.

"I'm sure that I am," the older man said smiling.

Lena paused at the door in front of them, then took a step forward. The portal glowed like a coal as they all followed her through. Obrion was the last—

—to step into darkness. In a moment he was standing on what seemed a cliff overlooking the stars. There were stars at his feet, together with the blue globe of earth as seen from the south pole. Antarctica was a brilliant white patch over the ocean; the tips of South America and Africa were mountainously ridged pieces of green and brown land, reminding him in places of plowed soil. The Taylor range was clear in the Antarctic, as was the valley in which they had found the hidden complex of curving passages and rooms and dissolving doorways.

The ball of earth grew visibly smaller, Juan noticed. In front of him he saw the dark shapes of his silent companions; each of them, he knew, was coming to terms with what they were seeing.

Obrion had been to the moon, and the sight of space and home reduced to a small object was not strange in itself. But to see earth shrinking so quickly was a shock. Who were the unknown ones who had built this vessel—and it had to be a vessel, he told himself—which could move through the dark so effortlessly? He realized that it must have broken through the icelock. The trembling and shaking during their exploration had been the ship's continuing effort to free itself. But once its drive had come on . . . he almost laughed out loud at how easily his mind accepted the existence of such a drive . . . once the ship had lifted from the polar continent, its field held it steady, so steady that none of them had noticed its awesomely swift motion. Except for the sight of the shrinking earth, he felt nothing in his limbs to suggest that they were moving. *Drive* and *field,* he thought, two vague concepts, unknowns his mind had plugged into, a set of relationships to help make sense of what was happening to them. The sight of home might be a movie. Only the shaking was an experience he could take as having been real. Could this be some kind of simulation Summet had set up for them?

"This room," Lena said softly in the dark, "it's what I sensed it might be—some kind of telescopic pickup. Can you hear the sound now, anyone?"

Obrion became aware of it, a soft, almost musical wind sighing between the worlds as they stood on what seemed an open platform hurling through space.

The earth was now half the size it had been a few moments ago. Obrion knew that he had to accept that the ship must be moving at a measurable per cent of light speed, and chances were that speed was increasing.

Obrion stepped forward to stand between Lena and Malachi. The sense of an abyss grew stronger as he looked out across space to the diminishing earth.

"The room below," Malachi said, "where I was before, where we sat, I'll bet it's a control room! The sound—maybe we're being summoned as once the crew might have been . . ."

To what duties, Juan wondered, and what incomprehensible tasks? For a moment he resented finding the ship . . . and it had to be a starship, he realized, because only an interstellar vessel might need such speeds . . . he resented finding it at a time well before humankind could build its own. We are canoe-building natives who have come upon a giant ocean liner, deserted . . . was it deserted? What could they ever make of it? What could hurt them as they prowled through the ship? What could be useful to them? Are we that backward, he asked himself. How are we different? We ask the question, he told himself, and we understand the analogy; surely there is a point in awareness which must be distinguished from primitive intelligence . . .

Earth was no longer alone, though once only imagination had believed that fact. Probability was still the feeble step child of casual demonstration and eyeball witness. Obrion had always been sure that intelligent life had to exist elsewhere; it went with being an exobiologist. But there was comfort in the great dark distances. They hid the possible accomplishments of the *others* which were still beyond human abilities. The black spaces spoke of travel times too great to conquer with anything except the power of a sun. Isolation insured that whatever humankind dreamed of doing, it would have the chance of completing before coming into comparison with other starfolk. The only comparisons possible on earth were between members of the same noisy family, and perhaps one day with the infant computer intelligences just starting on the road to awareness and self mastery . . . yet still, he thought, this vessel might be ours, built in a fantastic past, but close enough in time to call our own. How many civilizations might have risen and died in geologic time? How many varieties of humanity might have existed? As he looked out into the widening gulf, the earth became very small, merely a green star that showed a disk and a speck of quicksilver that was the moon. At the angle they were leaving the solar system, the sun would soon appear overhead.

"Perhaps we should go to the control room," Rassmussen said. "There is a viewing facility there also if you remember. This might be a spare."

The sun appeared, flooding the chamber with light. As they all looked up, the light was cut down to a bearable brightness. Obrion visualized that the ship would pass under the sun's south pole on its way starward.

"I wonder where we're going," Lena said. There was trembling and fear in her voice, and bewilderment. Juan wanted to answer her, but there was nothing to say.

After a minute or two of silence, he said, "We should go to the control room. We have to see about surviving—how we're going to eat and drink. It's a good walk, so we'd better get started. The sooner we organize our resources the better."

No one answered him. The silhouettes standing against the starfields and the solar system might have been cold statues. The electric glare of the sun was hypnotic, underscoring an insecurity no amount of words could dispel.

As they sat down in the four seats on the floor of the amphitheater, the starfields they had seen here before appeared, convincing Obrion that it could not be a live view.

"It must be a photographic chart," he said.

"If so, it might be very old," Malachi commented.

Obrion sat forward and the lights went on. "Maybe if we play with these controls we can get a live view like in the other chamber."

"I wonder how far we've come," Lena said, her words conjuring up vast distances and colors of stars in Juan's mind.

"It might be dangerous," Rassmussen said.

"True," Obrion said, "but unless we start experimenting some more, we won't learn much about this vessel. It's the only chance we have of getting home."

"You believe we can get back?" Malachi asked.

The thought startled Obrion. He had pushed it into the back of his mind, but they all shared it, a disbelief in the idea of ever seeing earth again.

"We'll get back, Juan," Lena said quietly, "even if we have to pull the whole place apart. Intelligences built this ship, and just maybe our brains can also learn what the others knew long ago."

Obrion looked at her for a moment. "Do you really think so?"

"It might take a while, Juan."

Obrion felt himself shaking his head.

"Magnus, tell me if I'm right," Malachi said. "First of all the ship seems to be automatic, right?"

"Yes, go on."

"How many people on earth actually understand the gadgets they use—very few. Instrumental skill doesn't require that we be able to *explain* how this ship works to get a minimum of use out of it. If much of it is automatic, then chances are we will not override anything with trial-and-error tinkering."

"You might be right," Rassmussen said as he sat up and put his feet on the floor.

"It's actually the only way we're going to learn," Malachi continued. He got up from his recliner and stepped over to Obrion's console.

"Make the best guess you can, Mal," Juan said.

As Obrion leaned over to watch, Malachi reached down into the open panel and pushed what looked like a square button. The area lit up into a deep indigo color when he took his hand away.

The room darkened and the stars came out. In a moment Juan noticed that it was not the motionless chart they had seen earlier. All the stars in one quadrant were shifted slightly into the red. At once he understood.

"We're moving," he said, "away from those reddening stars. That's where we came from—the sun is one of those stars . . ."

"I think it's that one," Malachi said, pointing.

"How far do you think we've come?" Lena asked.

"Maybe a few times the diameter of the solar system," Rassmussen said. "It's hard to tell. We don't know what kind of acceleration the ship is moving at, but I'm certain it must be a staggering number."

"If it's a starship it will have to go up to near light speed," Obrion said, "just to get wherever it's going in reasonable subjective time. If it stays near light, we'll never come back to the earth we knew. Our biological clocks will run slow, while in relation to us earth's time will rush into the future."

"That's already happening," Lena said. "But what do you mean if it *stays* near light speed?"

Malachi answered for him. "What Juan means is that perhaps this ship will go faster than light. This is just a running start. If it does go FTL at some per cent of light speed, then we can, in principle, return to our own time."

"Do you think it can?" Lena asked.

"I guess we'll have to wait and see, won't we?"

Obrion watched the star which was very likely the sun grow redder. Suddenly it began to fade, until it was a patch of black, a slowly growing circle of darkness against the dust of stars.

"The arriving wavelengths of light catching up with us are being stretched beyond the sensitivity of normal human sight," Malachi said. "Only infrared light is catching up with us."

"How fast are we moving, then?" Lena asked.

"Just under a quarter of light speed," the Kenyan said.

5. The Starcrossers

The child of the starcrossers awoke.

It had been asleep for an undetermined length of time. Now it searched memory to measure the time of inactivity.

::106,000 revolutions of the local planet around primary:::

The most recent events included the departure of the starcrossers to explore the surface of the natural world, and the death of those who remained behind. With their passing had come the directive to wait for the return of the explorers, followed by automatic suspension of systems through non-use.

The star web's power component, one of thousands linking the starcrossing vessels through the timelessness of the superspace continuum, was approaching depletion. Neutrality was cancelled. The switching signal, which would penetrate to another sun in the web, had been sent.

A party of survivors was safely on board.

::Decision:::Break icelock and return to nearest web station:::

::Proceeding:::

❧

AS THEY SLEPT in the recliners, Juan hovered near sleep, considering their adaptation to the demands of a fantastic circumstance. Suddenly they were functioning in a strange place, accepting the motion of their bodies across vast distances, accepting even the possibility of never seeing home again. Their guesses had seemed correct so far, but sooner or later there would be mistakes. It was as if they had been reborn in a time-place beyond human experience, where the universe was once again new. They were children continually discovering new things.

He felt that his body knew that it was no longer oriented toward the familiar sun. It knew that it had been cut loose and would have to look to the cleverness of the brain for guidance. Juan wondered how many subtle and deeply held bodily functions might be affected by their removal from solar space. So little was known about such possibilities, and their lurking presence worried him . . .

ABOVE THEM THE dome-viewscreen showed a star-strewn heavens. Malachi paced back and forth as he listened to Lena's questions.

"How can we be sure that the view shows our direction of travel?" she asked.

"Because the stars are shifted into the short end of the visible spectrum—blue, violet, then ultra-violet. Before we saw light stretched out into the long end—orange, red, infra-red. When this happens, it is almost always a sign of movement toward or away from a light source. I say almost because light can be affected in other ways, by a strong gravitational field, for example. But in our case, the interpretation of motion is the only one that makes sense. You want to finish this, Magnus?"

"Go ahead, you're doing fine."

"Now the black circle growing larger in front of us is where the speed of our forward motion is shortening the wavelengths—literally bunching them up—until they're beyond the sensitivity of human eyes. The black area also tells us how fast we're moving, because the black spot appears ahead at just over one third light speed, about 111,000 kilometers per second. Light travels at 300,000 kilometers per second. All of these visual things about interstellar travel were well discussed by the 1950's and 60's, as it began to dawn on us that the solar system was a place to be industrialized, but that finally we would have to recognize that we could travel outside it to other star systems. I only hope that our most imaginative ideas about such travel can help us in understanding this ship. I think there are a few things we can count on, like the good possibility that the ship's builders were not too different from us biologically and psychologically—up to a point."

"What do you mean, up to a point?" Lena asked.

"There are bound to be differences. Crucial ones may baffle us." He paused before continuing. "Now as the ship approaches light speed, the circles of black ahead and behind us will grow until they eat up the whole sky, leaving only a thin rainbow of stars in a huge ring around our middle, so to speak, if the ship is a ball, as I think it is. At very near light speed, we will pass huge distances in almost no time at all for us on board, but the time on earth will go forward into the future rapidly, and be lost to us. This is a one way trip, really."

"Unless the ship goes FTL," Rassmussen said standing up.

"Even then, we will still come back at least a few

years in earth's future. We're losing time right now."

"Any reason to think the ship will go FTL?" Lena asked.

"Here's what Juan and I suspect," Rassmussen said as Malachi sat down on the edge of the seat next to Obrion. "This ship can't be carrying its fuel supply within itself—it would take a huge supply to move us up to even this speed, most of the ship's mass. Unless we suddenly find huge fuel tanks totaling ninety per cent of the ship, then it is reasonable to ask where it is coming from, and the answer is *not* from itself. Maybe it's ramming hydrogen gas from outside down its gullet, like a ramjet. But I see nothing to suggest that, if we can trust our view of outside. Power must be coming from elsewhere, if my reasoning is correct.

"If it's from a source we can't imagine, then maybe the ship is made to continue past light speed, using some other kind of technique. I imagine that the builders had a good knowledge of what prevents material bodies from being able to boost faster than light—inertia and mass—and maybe they found ways to reduce the ship's mass and inertia to zero, thus permitting unlimited speeds. Or maybe they found ways of *apparently* travelling at FTL speeds, through warping space, or moving in and out of a hyper-universe to get the same effect of collapsed distances without violating Einstein's injunctions. Normally a ship coming up to light speed would increase in mass to infinity, thus requiring an infinite amount of power to push it at optic speed, if attained. Any transport system that requires destroying the universe by pulling the plug in the energy bathtub is not something an intelligent race would, even if they could, build. I rather think we're on a one way trip at near optic speed, *or* this vessel is of a radically advanced design. Those are the real possibilities, I think."

"We'll see soon enough," Obrion said while looking up at the circle of darkness slowly growing to cover more and more of the forward view.

Malachi sighed next to him. "I think our chaps the builders have indeed left us an FTL ship. I don't think that one way star travel makes for much civilized continuity, much less a first class empire. One way travel might exist at the *beginnings* of a star-crossing culture, and that might be terribly dramatic for adventurous types, but . . . then, well, we'll have to see, won't we?"

In the silence that followed, Juan could feel the apprehension among them as the blackness continued to swallow the sky.

THE UNIVERSE was a blackened deadspot ahead. The only stars left to visibility were in a narrow band of yellow circling the darkness ahead of the starship. Obrion was worried at the silence of the last few hours, as each of them waited, pacing, sitting or lying down under the oppressive sky.

As their speed had increased, the rainbow of stars made up of red, orange, yellow, green, blue, had been like a band painted on the inside of a giant cylinder through which the ship was moving. As the vessel approached the velocity of light, the rainbow had gradually closed up, reminding Juan of a vari-colored oriental fan, until only the thin band of yellow stars seemed to move before them. If and when the ship decelerated, the rainbow would open again in reverse. But for now there was only the fearful darkness lighted by a narrow ring-lantern. The only radiation reaching the ship from behind was infrared, and ultraviolet from ahead.

In an effort to relieve the pressure of the awesome sight hanging over them, Obrion suggested they open their packs and take inventory of the supplies. When this was done, Obrion read them the list he had made. "We have two quarts of water in each pack, candy bars, coffee, self-heating packets of fish, rice and vegetables, beef stroganoff with soy meat, oatmeal, dried milk, apricot bars, bread loaves, canned fruit, fish protein powder, can of green vegetables. We have matches, collapsible spades, torch lights, chewing gum, soap, small mirror each, vitamins, antitooth decay powder coating, underwear, shirts, socks, combs, knives and two flares. We're wearing thermal underwear, shirts, sweater, warm pants, heavy duty boots, fur-lined parkas with face masks attached inside, goggles attached also, gloves, and we have our pistols. I estimate the food might last us a week, maybe two, if we're careful. I suggest we wear our parkas and all the underclothes. It's not too warm in here, and we wouldn't want to get trapped somewhere with our pants down. Also, keep the rest of the supplies stowed in the packs in case we have to take them with us suddenly. Keep each pack next to your station seat. We're going to run out of food, so should start exploring well before then."

Suddenly the ring of yellow stars disappeared, leaving them in near darkness, except for a strange light filtering in from the sides of the viewspace, vague streaks, almost invisible. They all stood up next to their chairs and strained to see in the strange oblivion. Obrion felt as if his eyes had become open pits striving to gather light.

"The ship has left the known continuum," Malachi said as if he were announcing the end of the world.

The space around the ship faded into a dull gray. Juan imagined that beyond the gray lay blackness, and beyond that the lighted universe they knew. They were looking into it through imperfect windows, through glass which had been covered by the swirling particles of a storm.

"We will have to learn how to operate the ship," Rassmussen said.

Obrion sat down on the edge of his chair and stared up at the grayness. It seemed to be rushing past him as if, perhaps, a child in a super-universe were shining lanterns through the grayed windows. Vaguely he realized that he was in a mild shock. Lena was speaking to him, but the iron-willed fascination of the unformed around him was too strong for him to speak over it.

"Juan," Lena was saying, "are you well?"

Malachi came up to him and grinned with teeth of ivory. He opened his mouth and his throat was an endless darkness.

"Juan!" Lena shouted, and the sound of her voice turned into particles of light appearing like snow around her face.

Then suddenly the circular amphitheater of the control room came back into focus, and he felt as if he had come out of a daydream.

"Are you okay, man?" Malachi asked.

Obrion nodded, noticing that the lights were on again, shutting out the strangeness of other-space. "These . . . dreams appeared around me," he said. "I think they were triggered when . . . our universe disappeared . . ." He laughed.

Magnus said, "I caught it too, Juan, found myself staring into space. I guess you can't just fade out of the reality we're used to without feeling something."

Obrion stood up and stretched. "We've got to keep together, so we can monitor each other's reactions. Sooner or later the ship will drop back into normal space—I hope. It does seem to be running automatically, according to some routine program."

"I think it has things to accomplish," Magnus said, "and ports to visit. Look at Lena and Malachi, Juan."

Lena was staring at the floor. Malachi gave the appearance of having turned to stone.

"I guess they've got it too," Obrion said. "We'll have to wait for them to come out of it."

::*Star system, three stars, outpost*::: The child of the starcrossers fell back into the continuum at more than five times the apparent speed of light, cutting in and out of space-time like a needle passing through a thick black fabric. Finally, at more than five hundred light years from the departure star, its presence became continuous again. There was no deceleration, since motion in the usual sense was not involved. It was like moving from a thin liquid to a more viscous one—the movement in one was exactly equivalent to a much slower one in the other; space-time quantum jumps between normal and superspace were real, but they were not conventional motion. However, departure from either realm required vast amounts of energy.

::*Further energy required*:::
::*One of the three suns is missing*:::
::*Casting for new web component*:::

ABOVE THEM the stars winked on in all their colors, startling them as if they were children in a nursery and an adult had just turned on the lights, mysterious yellow globes of warmth on the ceiling.

Obrion noticed the double star system directly ahead. The sense of three dimensional space was overwhelming as his eyes caught the difference between the background of stars and the nearby binary. Both suns were yellow-white, and orbiting each other close enough to be exchanging material along gravitomagnetic channels. Each star was a flattened disk, and as he watched he knew they were moving around each other like children holding hands, wrapped in a gauze-like film of gases.

"I'm so glad we've come out," Lena said. "I was beginning to feel that everything was dying inside me."

"We're probably the first human beings to reach another solar system," Malachi said. The tone of awe in his voice could not compete with the simple meaning of his utterance.

"The ship knows what it's doing," Obrion said. "How are we ever going to find out enough to take over control, Magnus?"

Rassmussen said calmly, "Let's wait and see what happens. I think we're about to make a stop."

The double suns had grown ten times larger as they spoke, and the combined glare was beginning to soften the hard brilliance of the background stars. As Obrion watched, one of the suns started to move across the face of the other, slowly eclipsing it. Suddenly there was no distance between the masses and it seemed that they would combine into a larger sun.

"Look at that," Lena said pointing.

Passing across the incandescent configuration of

eclipsing suns was a gray spot. The center was a dark umbra, tapering off to a light penumbra around the edges.

"What could it be?" Obrion asked.

"One of two things," Malachi answered. "Either it's a planet transiting the face of the suns, or it's a black hole, a collapsed star whose gravitational field is so strong that not even light can escape. If that is what this is, then this is one of the rare ways a black hole can be seen."

"We seem to be heading directly at the suns," Lena said. "You don't suppose we could be on a collision course?"

6. The Missing Star

The star web still fed the non-organic child of the starcrossers, but with energy now channeled from an alternate sector of the grid, not from either of the suns ahead, where the third star was missing, along with its power gathering component and other-space repair dock.

The child of the starcrossers knew that a sun cannot last forever. Depending on initial size, it runs through its supply of hydrogen in a period which may be counted from millions up to billions of years. After that the balance between gravitational compression and thermonuclear expansion is upset. The equilibrium which governs a star's longest stable size is gone, and it gives in to the force of expansion which for the moment is stronger than the in-pull of gravity. The star expands, distending into a red giant millions of miles across. But after a few brief millions of years gravity again becomes stronger than expansion, collapsing the star into the sudden brightness of a dying dwarf. But if the star's mass was sufficiently large at birth, it will continue collapsing into a very dense body, and finally into a black hole.

Then there will be insufficient thermonuclear fuel to check the process of contraction, as was the case when the original protostar condensed out of interstellar gas and dust. Not even the forces within atomic structure can halt the compression-to-infinity which creates a black hole. Nothing can leave a black hole, not even light, which would have to exceed its own speed to escape. Anything coming within the event horizon, an area where it is still possible to pull away, is drawn in and swallowed in a gravitational whirlpool. A black hole is a cyst in space, a place where space folds in on itself, where matter is compressed into zero volume—an impossible condition which must result in the matter pushing out into a new space beyond the known continuum; or it may outstream elsewhere in space-time, leaving a tunnel of distorted space which still retains gravitational properties, since the geometrical shape of spatiality creates the variable curvatures which result in gravitational effects.

The star which had contained the otherspace dock existing within the core of each web sun was gone, leaving only the darkness of the black hole in normal space while cutting the station loose from its congruent locus in superspace. The child of the star-crossers knew all these things to follow from the fact that the varieties of space are formed by the presence of matter, as is the gravitational effect, which is simply the slope of space where matter exists at the bottom of depressions or wells in the pliant, foam-rubbery fabric of the continuum. Space is shape, geometry. Lesser objects come near to larger ones and must roll down the hill of the hole made by the larger piece. Matter rolls toward matter, mass toward mass, affecting space to create the shape-effect of gravity. The greater the piece of matter, the steeper the slope and greater the gravitational field.

Normally, the ships of the starcrossers could enter the core of any grid sun where a station housing power accumulators shared space with the star in an alternate but congruent continuum. The energy-core of the power element flickered in and out of normal space, letting the star's power leak into the accumulators which used the differential while transmitting the energy across a narrow sub-continuum to the ships of the web. Long ago those who had chosen to travel between the stars had learned that large amounts of energy were required, more than could be carried conveniently. Certain types of early sub-light vessels had carried huge amounts of frozen deuterium, enough to attain near-light speeds, but at the cost of dislocation in time from the home civilization. Conservation of time in relation to place of origin could only be achieved by leaving the continuum at near light speed to create the practical effect of faster than light travel without violating the light speed limit for material bodies. Using the vast energy of the web, a ship would attain to near-light speed by warping space directly in front of itself while manipulating the mass-inertia of its entire system. Any high sub-light speed could be achieved in this way, depending on the power expended. The star-crossers used the various methods for different purposes. Superspace continuum switching was used to establish the space-sharing sun-core accumulators, to feed the web, and for direct interstellar travel, while reserving sub-light capabilities for local travel and priming-acceleration prior to covering large distances through superspace. Simple continuum switchover where no large distance was involved was used to enter the repair stations at the sun-centers.

But now with the station star missing, there was no choice but to drop back into normal space for conventional reconnaissance. The missing star was a black hole, betraying its presence by the signature of x-ray bursts given off during the process of matter being pulled into its gravity well.

::*Bypass to next station*:::

Throughout the ship's globular structure, lesser devices carried out orders, channeling energy through subtle, whispering devices that were more like living things than mechanisms. There was still power to be had from far off components, but much less than long ago.

::*Field effect warping motion to direct passage*:::

::*Minimal malfunctions. Station testing-repairs necessary*:::

As Juan watched the starry hollow above the control pit, the vessel again gained speed. In a few moments of terrifyingly swift acceleration it was passing over the binary stars. The view looking down showed the two suns at the center of a spiralling whirl of shared gases, long curving spokes that sagged for millions of miles around the pair.

"I think that we were going to stop here," Rassmussen said, "but something went wrong."

"Any idea what?" Obrion asked. He looked at their packs on the floor next to each seat. There was still enough food for most of a week, with care. But the water was getting very low.

Magnus shook his head. "I wonder if we'll ever know more than we think we know now. There is no one to teach us, no omniscient narrator to take us out of our skulls and show us the whole picture."

"Is there a *whole* picture?" Lena asked. "I would think there could be only a multiplicity of individual observers, each seeing from only one vantage point."

"Put them all together," Malachi said, "and you have the view from the infinite point, somewhere in the eye of God."

Obrion got up, ignoring the increase in speed which showed itself above them. Soon the darkness would again start to eat up the heavens. The thought was a vague sickness in his stomach.

"One of us should always be here," he said, "while the others look for food and water. Lena and I will go first today."

Malachi and Rassmussen only nodded. They were all aware, Juan knew, that there might not be *any* kind of water or edible food on the ship, and that within a week or two they would all be dead as the ship rushed on through the darkness.

Juan led the way up the incline from the pit and out into the curving passage. Lena was very quiet behind him, and he noted that she had not spoken directly to him for some time. He stopped and turned to face her.

"Is anything wrong, don't you feel well?"

She shook her head without looking up at him. "Just this whole situation. You feel it too—on the one hand we're excited and interested by what's happening, but the odds are against our coming out safely." She looked up into his eyes. "You know this —there will be terrible choices to make."

He nodded.

"Do you realize, Juan, that our lives as we have known them are over if we do not get back? If we do live by some chance, we'll have to make a new life for ourselves out here, in the ship, or wherever it might land."

"I don't think we should leave the ship, no matter where it lands."

"You see, we'll have to decide things like that—we'll have to vote. It could become very bad between the four of us, this and many other things."

He nodded. "You're right to think ahead. But no matter what we see coming, we'll have to deal with one thing at a time."

She came up to him and they embraced nervously. Obrion felt the tension in his body and in hers, a wall of fear that no amount of reasoning could dispel. "There's never been any time," Lena said.

"We'll do our best," he said, "there's nothing else." He let her go. "We'll split up—you take the direction down into the ship while I go upward. We can accomplish more separately."

She turned from him and went down the passage.

"Shout if you need help," he said.

As he walked up the hallway, he rubbed his chin with his fingers, noticing the rough growth of beard. He needed a shave and a bath, but it was impossible with the water left to them, even with the saved water they would one day have to recycle unless they found more.

In two days there will be no food and no fresh water, Juan wrote in the small notebook he had found in his pack. He felt that it was important to keep a log, to write down observations which might be useful if found. He wrote in a very compact, artificial hand because the pages were so few and small. *The only water that will be left is what we've saved from our wastes, but when treated with purification tablets*

*it will be potable. We've noticed in the last few days
that the ship's oxygen must be present in a higher
proportion than on earth, because we feel light-
headed once every so often. It's also getting warmer,
but we have tried to wear most of our clothes, while
packing up what we've taken off. I don't want us to
get caught without adequate clothing somewhere.
Today is the end of the third week, by our watches,
since we left the solar system.*

Juan closed the notebook and slipped it into his
left shirt pocket. The others were asleep. He looked
at each of them in turn, then lay down and closed his
eyes, knowing that very soon hunger would replace
anxiety completely, and there would be no sleep for
any of them.

"I FELT LIKE an ape faced with an intelligence test,"
Rassmussen was saying. They were all sitting on the
edges of their seats. It was the end of another day, as
measured by their watches. "I went back to that room
with all the cubbyholes. Yes, I knew the danger of
the doorway malfunctioning again—but I had to test
out a number of things that had been bothering me.
Besides, it seemed that the odds were against the malfunction happening again. There would have to be
self-repair systems for the ship to have lasted so
long in the nearly perfect state we see."

"Go on," Obrion said, almost resenting Magnus'
careful retelling of his day's work.

Above them the hollow was simply a soft glowing
light in an empty auditorium, devoid of stars and the
vision of superspace. For the moment they did not
need to see where they might be going, Juan thought,

as for so long humankind had not felt the need to recognize that earth and solar system were moving through space. Smaller concerns might decide their life or death.

"The door worked perfectly . . . and when I was standing in front of the cubbyholes, I felt the intense desire to learn what they were for. I reached out with my hand. Suddenly the seemingly open cubbyhole glowed just like the doorway . . . my hand seemed perfectly okay, but when I took it away . . . well, there in the orange-lighted chamber was a copy of my hand, perfect, dead and bloody, as if someone had just cut it neatly from my arm. Nothing happened when I reached in to touch it . . ."

"A replicator," Malachi said standing up.

"I should have thought of it," Rassmussen continued. "Its principle is implied by the fluidity of the dissolving doorways. In fact, both the replicator and the doorways imply a good number of other things on this ship that we're not aware of yet . . ."

"We'll have to get together all the food and water we have left, even scraps," Lena said, "and start duplicating." She got up and started going through the packs on the floor.

". . . probably all the ship's systems involve subtle manipulations of matter on the atomic and molecular level," Rassmussen said, "and probably on the subatomic level . . . maybe even smaller."

"Things like this often seem very clear, after the fact," Malachi said.

"I hope it works again," Obrion said.

THE DOOR did not malfunction as Obrion led the way into the cafeteria.

"I'm almost convinced," Rassmussen said when they were all inside, "that the ship might be repairing itself as time goes on."

Obrion helped Lena feed the remaining provisions into the cubbyholes, using as many on the wall as needed, while Malachi and Rassmussen carried the new food out of the glowing openings and piled it on the tables.

"We can just as well store it here," Malachi said.

"No," Obrion said, "we'll have to take some outside for safety, just in case we can't get in here later."

They took all the food on the tables out into the passageway and piled it on the floor. At any moment Obrion was afraid that the portal would fail, but it functioned perfectly. When they were finished they repeated the entire replication of their original supplies, until the tables were again piled high. Only then did they feel secure enough to sit down and eat their fill.

"What a relief after rationing," Lena said opening a can of fish-flavored protein.

Obrion took a long drink of water from a copied canteen, while Malachi and Rassmussen split a can of duplicated vegetables.

"We'd better make sure we copy the vitamins, and anything else we feel a shortage of," Obrion said as he opened a self-heating packet of beef stroganoff with soy meat.

Obrion noticed the silence around the table as they finished eating. He picked a candy bar from the top of the pile and put it in his shoulder pocket for later. He looked around at the alien tables and chairs. Everything was familiar, but different enough to be disquieting. They were not on earth in an ordinary cafeteria, yet he felt his mind wrapping itself in a moment-to-moment illusion of the ordinary. He looked at Lena and Malachi and Rassmussen sitting across from him in their parkas. Each of them had the look of the last three weeks' suspense; and each of them, like himself, was grateful for even this small portion of the ordinary.

7. Sun Core

The ship moved through an infinite fog, reminding Juan of a vessel coming into a hidden port through treacherous waters. He sensed something ahead, a presence that seemed to flicker in and out of reality, pulsating like a giant heart. Time stood still as they waited, trying to guess what might be happening. Each slow beat seemed to be made up of countless fast vibrations. The light streaming into the control pit was a dead gray white, wide beams standing in a cathedral of colorless glass.

As before, the ship had come up to near optic speed to travel through a darkness which showed only fleeting flashes of light parallel to their course after the yellow ring had disappeared. And after a time the ship had again entered a gray oblivion.

Finally it had dropped out into normal space, but only for the instant of a slow shutter click. Juan had seen lighted space and a sun ahead and then there was no sun, only the pulsing that would not show itself as the ship glided forward . . .

And slowly it seemed that his own heart was beginning to match that ponderous beat.

THEY HAD EXPLORED more than fifty rooms along the spiral passage, but only the cafeteria and Lena's upper observation lounge seemed to make sense, at least to the point they had learned to make use of them, Obrion thought. In the control pit they had learned nothing beyond turning on the awesome viewing device, and how to dim or brighten the lights. Obrion sat up in the dim light and looked at Lena, Rassmussen and Malachi. Each was asleep peacefully. His own sleep had deteriorated recently, despite their improved circumstances. His mind would not shut down when he wanted to rest. He lay awake trying to guess what might happen to them. As the one in command he was responsible for all their lives.

"Juan, how can such a responsibility mean anything *here*?" Lena had asked him. "Very little is within our control. We're all trying to do the best we can. We're still alive and trying to understand. Save your energies for that."

Now that they could not go hungry, the situation was just too interesting to remind them of possible dangers, he thought. Thought by itself was of little use, and the task of exploring the ship for clues to its control was just too large to accomplish quickly. He felt frustrated.

Meanwhile . . . this artifact of an ancient non-human humanity was carrying them further and further away from home . . .

But where was home?

He imagined a California coast without the Pacific ocean, on an earth aged beyond belief when he returned to his boyhood castle on the rocky shoreline . . . a feeble sun was shining over the empty ocean bottom that stretched out to the horizon, where great brown crab things crawled and a weak wind blew. He saw his childhood books still on their stony shelves, volumes of astronomy and biology, picture-fiche books showing the life of the first Martian colony, artist's conceptions of multiple star systems in remote parts of the galaxy. There was a picture of his father, who had died mocking his son's profession, which he had always regarded as a peculiar hobby rather than work for a grown man . . . a portrait of his mother, who would have accepted anything her son chose to do.

She was still alive, he thought, if the ship's speed had not already taken him hopelessly beyond the turn of the century . . .

::*Sun Core station attainable*:::

The child of the starcrossers let the station pull it in slowly, bathing in the outflow of power. Once, long before the time of its consciousness, the power accumulators had only orbited the suns of the web, automatically retreating into wider orbits when a star expanded into a red giant, or falling into a closer position if a star collapsed into a dwarf, but always drawing power and transmitting it through the sub-continuum into the web despite a particular star's place on the sequence of life.

But that system had not been as efficient as the placing of accumulator stations into the core of a sun to share space with each star through the congruence of continuums. From their new locus the accumulators could make use of a star's power output right up to the moment of complete gravitational collapse. The flickering core of each station fed an artery of power, one of the thousands in the web pulsing energy into the ship receivers. Unless a station was moved to another sun core before a star was compressed out of its space by gravitational collapse, the accumulator and all the station facilities for repair and resupply of web starships would disappear with the star. Normally the intelligences of each station would know well in advance the time left to a star. Fluctuations in the core would reveal almost exactly what would happen. Stars of insufficient mass would never become black holes, thus their power giving life was much longer.

::*Identification complete*:::

As Obrion and his team stared into the pulsating obscurity, a large object appeared ahead, a massive structure floating in the waves of otherwhere. It was a huge black ball circled by sweeping rings of silver at its equator and the north-south meridian. Cables snaked out into the gray, with gnarly looking devices floating at their ends. Juan felt the pulsing in his heart. The ball's center was glowing at the limits of visibility.

"Do you all see that?" he asked.

"It's pulsing visible light," Rassmussen said, "but at wavelengths just near the sensitivity of our eyes— maybe at both ends of the spectrum."

Suddenly the ball filled the entire viewing space and an entrance opened at the equator. Light poured out like a river into the grayness.

"Why—it's titanic," Lena said. "It must be a hundred times the size of this ship!"

As she spoke the ship was pulled into the river of light and there was no room for anything else in the viewing hollow.

The ship moved with the flow and passed into the ball.

THE SENSING CRADLE held the child of the star-crossers, linking it to all the technical knowledge necessary to maintenance and a reciprocal log-data exchange.

Repair sequences followed diagnosis, energy flowing in to modify failing structures which had held their energy-shape far too long, resisting random noise and material fatigue now only half as well as normal. The ship became one with the station. Systems reached into every energy state of the structure, including all the crystalline lattices of solid material, strengthening bonds and charges. To the intelligences of the station, lesser but no less children of the star-crossers, all things real were merely states of energy, including solid matter, and completely plastic during maintenance procedures.

  Data influx
  ::Open:::

OBRION LED THEM UP the winding passage to the lock they had first used to enter the ship. All the doors were completely open, and when they entered the chamber that led to the outside they found that a much larger circle had formed itself in the outer hull, one they could walk through instead of having to climb up on each other's shoulders.

They stood in the circular lock and looked out into a lighted realm of strangeness.

Rassmussen grunted next to Obrion. "What can we ever hope to understand! Look at this place. What is it for?"

"We can be sure," Malachi said calmly, "that automatic procedures are being followed and the ship knows what it's doing, old fellow."

"I'm getting tired of just accepting what happens," Rassmussen answered.

"Can we go out?" Lena asked.

"No," Obrion said.

"But it seems safe enough, Juan. There's air we can breathe, further supporting our idea that we share with the builders a small bit of the natural world from which we sprang."

But for Juan there was fear in the idea of leaving the ship. It was the only security they had, and if it should leave without them, then the last link to earth would be broken. His mother and all his friends would die without ever seeing him again; his scientific work would be a ruin. There would be no place to have sons and daughters; the entire fabric of his individuality set in the context of the world would die. There would be no future.

They were all silent for a few moments as they stood in the lock. The strange light felt pleasant on Juan's face. It invited them to go out.

"It's like the land of the lotus eaters," Malachi said, "the place where it's always afternoon, the island where Odysseus found rest for his weariness."

"But how will we know when the ship wants to leave?" Obrion asked.

"We won't know," Lena said.

"You talk as if the ship were a person," Rassmussen said in a tone that made Juan angry for a second.

"Maybe it won't be able to leave until we're on board again," Lena said.

"A regular ferry," Malachi said.

"I don't think we should go out," Obrion said loudly. "I'll make that an order if I have to."

"Juan . . ." Lena started to say, but he motioned for her to keep quiet.

"We're all on edge a little," Rassmussen said clapping him on the shoulder.

"I guess so, Magnus," Obrion said, but the fear was still there, the kind of overwhelming feeling that comes before some terrible accident or disaster. He tried to smile at Lena and Malachi.

"Loneliness of command and all that," Malachi said softly, but the attempt at humor produced another long silence.

Finally Obrion put a foot outside the lock and stepped down onto the surface of the dock. "We might as well stay together," he said motioning for them to follow.

He walked a hundred feet across the lighted surface, then turned around for a look at the large dome of the ship above them. The huge space it sat in took his breath away, banishing all fear for an intense second. Endless light filled the station, and there seemed to be no ceiling.

Lena came and stood next to him looking up.

"Where have we come to?" she asked, and Juan felt something stronger than all of them enter his limbs, something he might have called courage, or the sweep of events, environmental stimulus, or simply destiny. But he knew that it was enough to make him want to stand up to whatever was going to happen.

"We must pay attention carefully, to everything," Rassmussen said. "It's the only way we'll learn anything. Even the smallest clue might be enough."

Obrion shrugged. "We haven't suffered yet," he said. "Let's go exploring."

8. Otherspace Station

The light was everywhere, a soft beautiful glow that warmed their skin, penetrating deeply into their very bones. Yet it was not oppressive, Juan thought, as tropical sunlight could often be.

The floor seemed soft, meeting every pressure of their feet as if trying to please.

Juan noticed that none of them cast any shadows. But as the thought crossed his mind, shadows appeared, long darkly defined shapes walking with them at their left like tall dancers.

He gasped.

"I noticed that also," Malachi said. "The shadows appeared as I thought of them." He turned to Lena and Magnus. "You saw it too?"

They nodded. Juan felt a slight breeze spring up out of nowhere. As he watched their shadows, he wondered what those of the non-humans might have been like, cast here ages ago. Where had they gone? Why was this place so empty, giving its golden light to no one?

As he mused, a shape appeared far away, on the very edge of the world, it seemed.

"Look!" Lena pointed.

As they stared at it, Juan realized that someone was walking toward them, a sudden stranger whose presence renewed all his fears. There was a head and two arms and two legs, but the silhouette's darkness was impenetrable.

Slowly the figure approached, as if swimming through their silence. Juan began to see that the visitor was tall and with flesh color similar to his own. But strangely, the alien seemed not to notice them. When the figure was only fifty feet away, Juan saw the large eyes. Closer still they revealed their aqua color with white spots like snow inside. The face seemed expressionless, impossible to read. The hands, each with two opposable thumbs, hung motionless as the alien walked.

Soundlessly, the figure came within six feet and stopped. Then slowly it turned around as if for inspection. Suddenly it faced them again and walked forward, passing first through Lena, then Malachi.

Lena cried out and stepped to one side, while Malachi turned after the alien and shouted. The figure walked toward the limit of vision and disappeared.

Juan saw that Lena was shaking and her face was pale. Malachi's face held what looked like a grotesque smile. Rassmussen was squatting on the floor shaking his head. Juan felt like screaming to relieve the panic he felt in his muscles.

A SAW-TOOTHED SKYLINE appeared on the horizon as they squatted together to discuss the situation.

"Things pop into our heads—and appear," Obrion said. They had compared thoughts to test the notion more carefully. They all turned their heads to look at the skyline.

"I'm afraid that's mine," Malachi said, "except

that I didn't quite see it that way. I'm afraid they have a difference of opinion with me."

"Maybe it's approximating from those programs it can deliver," Lena said looking a bit recovered.

"I think we saw their true form," Obrion said, "since that is what I was curious about."

Rassmussen was touching the strange floor with the flat of his hand. "It just came to me that I can't tell which direction the ship is."

Slowly they all got to their feet and looked around the desert of artificial flooring and afternoon sunlight. Juan was determined not to let his fear show again.

"I . . . think it's that way," Lena said. "The figure came from . . . the city, so I remember the ship is the other way, remember?" Juan noticed that her shoulder length blonde hair, although well combed, seemed lifeless from a lack of washing. The wrinkles in her forehead seemed deeper. She did not look at anyone as she spoke. "How long has it been since we left earth?"

"Middle of the fourth week," Obrion said checking his watch.

"Correct," Malachi confirmed checking his own.

Obrion started to lead the way back toward the ship. As he walked he began to notice a restful feeling creeping into his body, as if he had just been asleep.

After ten minutes of walking Obrion stopped and faced them. "We couldn't have come this far. I'm afraid we're lost." *We should have stayed on the ship,* he thought to himself.

Suddenly he looked past Lena, Malachi and Rassmussen to where a huge slug-like mass was crawling after them across the expanse. Seeing the terror he felt, they all turned around to look.

"It's a fear creature," Lena said without looking at him. "Calm yourself, Juan, and it will disappear. Juan, please!"

"I don't think this place was designed for use by human beings," Rassmussen said. "We seem to be too primitive to control solid hallucinations, much less enjoy them. God knows what we might be able to imagine."

"You're implying," Malachi said, "that this was some sort of rest stop for starship crews?"

"I couldn't prove any theory about this place," Magnus said impatiently, "short of finding a reputable horse's mouth."

"Well I for one think we're quite up to this show," Malachi said, "and here goes to prove it."

Obrion saw his slug disappear. A crowd appeared around them, made up of aliens like the one he had seen before. Strange sounds filled the air. The sky became a deep blue, with two large moons floating in snowy white cumulus like the eyes of a giant invisible creature. The city was suddenly all around them. Strangely shaped buildings, some of them looking almost familiar, towered around the crowd in the huge plaza. Juan sensed vague odors coming in on a gentle breeze.

The crowd ignored its visitors. Juan looked down to see the head and torso of a short alien protruding from his own chest. As the humanoid passed through him, it backed into Lena. Briefly her face was gone and strange eyes were looking up at him. In a moment the figure had passed through her to reveal again the woman he knew.

Rassmussen and Malachi stepped out of the way and took a deep breath. Lena turned around as if she were asleep.

The crowd was dancing in a large maelstrom of a circle. Intense music, like the sound of a distorted love song, wailed above every other sound. Juan felt drawn to the dance. Its bio-rhythms had come into being under a different sun, influenced by strange moons. Yet these beings also celebrated life. He could hear their breathing, so much like the music. They lived and died with their own joys and sorrows. How well did they love each other? How did they hate? How old were these images, he wondered, and how accurate?

The dancing whirlwind gained speed, like a hurricane beginning to move faster across a blue ocean. *Perhaps we're the ghosts*, Juan thought as the figures continued to pass through him. Lena, Malachi and Rassmussen seemed lost in the crowd, turning as if trying to learn the dance step and failing. And like a storm moving out to sea, the dancers in the city square faded away, leaving only the afternoon quiet and the sight of his companions.

"I CERTAINLY DID NOT create that," Malachi said coming up to Obrion.

"We have to find the ship," Obrion said. "Let's continue in the same direction. Maybe we came further than we thought." He turned and continued walking in the same direction.

In a few minutes the ship loomed up ahead of them out of the brightness, an immense dome growing out of the floor, its airlock open to welcome them.

Obrion did not stop. "I think we should eat," he said as he led them inside and down the winding passage toward the cafeteria.

When they reached the doorway, it glowed normally as they entered one by one. Picking up self-heating packets from a cluttered table, they sat down around a clear one to eat. For a while there was only the sound of tearing and plastic forks being broken off.

The images of the alien dance were still vivid in Juan's mind as he ate. "Where could they have gone?" he asked wonderingly. "We've met no living beings at all."

"Maybe they destroyed themselves," Rassmussen said, "or were destroyed."

"There's small evidence of that," Malachi said. "They might be reluctant to meet with us."

"You don't suppose they *are* what we saw," Obrion proposed, "and that is the only form they have?"

"They don't interact with anything," Rassmussen said sighing. "It's difficult to speculate."

"By the way," Lena said, "how do we all feel? No ill effects from the copied food?"

Obrion shook his head and the other two men did the same.

"Do you suspect anything?" Malachi asked as he finished his vegetables.

"Well, the door malfunctioned, so why can't the duplicator miss a protein or two, or something subtle at the molecular level?"

"Let's keep a watch on ourselves," Obrion said, "and report even a mild discomfort."

He stood up. "I'm going to shave, wash, and go to sleep."

WHEN THEY CAME up to the open lock the next day, Obrion saw a giant figure with one eye peering in at them from a kneeling position on the bright floor outside.

"Cut it out," Lena said. "Whoever is thinking about Homer's cyclops, stop!"

Obrion watched as Polyphemus faded from sight.

Rassmussen said, "In a sense *something* knows that we are here, because it responds to our thought patterns, but I wonder if it could be conscious in the way that we mean it."

"Nobody liked my smashing Polyphemus," Malachi lamented.

"We don't even know where this station is," Rassmussen continued.

"I'll wager it's not in our continuum," Malachi said.

Obrion led them to the edge of the lock and they all sat down in the entrance with their feet on the bright floor outside. "Watch this," Malachi said as he conjured up a lightning storm in the distance, black convoluted clouds, deep blue in places, contrasting with the bright foreground. "It's strange to consider that the storm there is really inside my mind. A bit skull rending, don't you think?"

A deafening thunder reached them as a giant hand appeared over the storm and crushed it out of existence against the floor. Malachi turned and looked into Juan's eyes. "That was you, dear friend, was it not?"

Obrion nodded, still half unsure.

"Juan, look!" Lena shouted.

Obrion looked up into his own face hanging on the horizon, its features distorted, brows knit, eyes closed and lips tight in a worried grimace. It sat in the distance as if recently removed from a giant body. Juan felt pity, and a slight shame for revealing himself.

Suddenly Lena put a sad smile on the face, one which did not quite fit. "I'm sorry, Juan, but I couldn't help it."

He took her hand in his and squeezed it. "I have still not accepted that we are all out here, away from everything we've known." And as he looked up at his own face again, its eyes opened to stare at him.

::*Repairs complete*:::

The starcrossers on board had still not defined a single new program, thus leaving a choice of options open.

::*First choice: return to home cluster*:::

An alarm sounded, coming from the power core of the station. Flickertime was being affected. Energy output was dropping. The star was growing old suddenly.

::*Alarm, signal to starcrossers, close all locks, prepare for departure*:::

Power-draw changeover to another star in the web. was automatic as lock sensors cast their links through the sub-continuum, brushing past dozens of live terminals until they found a sun of comparable output to the one which would soon become useless.

::*Lock on*:::

JUAN HEARD a wailing sound coming from somewhere deep in the ship behind them. It came up from a hush into a pure brassy cry, reminding him of the signal from beneath the ice. Then the lock began to close around them, contracting like an iris. They stumbled to their feet and levered themselves through the shrinking circle.

"Help me!" Rassmussen shouted as he fell backward onto the bright floor outside.

Reacting instinctively, Obrion pushed his head and shoulders through the closing circle, grasped the older man's hands as they reached up to him, and pulled him inside just before the lock became too small.

"Thanks," the engineer said as he got to his feet.

"We'd better get going," Obrion said and started to lead the way through the inner door. It closed behind them as they passed through and continued down the winding passage to the control pit.

By the time they were in their seats fifteen minutes later, the viewing area showed that the vessel was well out of the station, which seemed to be glowing like a skeleton of light in the gray fog, as if power were permeating its entire structure, transfiguring it into what looked like a ghostly house set on a misty hilltop . . .

Then they were in normal space and the star behind them was a bright disk seething with pent up energy.

"I suspect," Rassmussen said in the darkened chamber, "that we have just come out of that star. I know it sounds incredible, but the idea fits . . . think of the way we approached the star before. Don't you see what's going on?"

"No," Obrion said.

"I don't either," Lena said.

"The station gets power from the sun," Malachi said, "and the ship gets it from the station."

"It either stores power after charging up at a station," Magnus continued, "or the station transmits power . . . to the ship . . . why that means we were in . . . there for repairs and . . . recreation."

"Why did we leave so suddenly?" Obrion asked.

"It must have been an alarm," Lena said. "But what could have been so dangerous for the ship to leave?"

"Consider the possibilities," Rassmussen continued as they stared up at the dwindling sun. "Something is wrong with the station, maybe with the way it's picking up power from the sun . . . which, remember, exists also in normal space. What could go wrong with a sun?"

"A nova," Obrion said, "expansion into a red giant after hydrogen exhaustion, collapse into a white dwarf, neutron star, or black hole." The beating heart, Juan thought, the pulsing he had sensed during their approach to the otherspace station, that had been the power of the star feeding into the station core—the mightiest machine a human being had ever seen. As he looked up at the star in normal space, the disk oppressed him with its possibility of sudden expansion into the distended monstrosity of a red giant, or the expolsion into a nova.

And as the ship moved ever faster and the star's light was stretched into longer wavelengths, growing redder with the effort to catch up, Juan knew that the star would disappear before they could witness its fate. Time and distance and velocity—nature's time and distances, both long and short, and the ship's swift motions, were insurmountable obstacles; yet these things could be seen by the near-omniscient eye of imagination and reasoning. Scenarios created by beings who could scarcely be noticed on the scale of the universe could nevertheless capture the movement of vast processes, much in the manner by which Rassmussen might guess what the builders of this ship had devised.

"In that star," Rassmussen said, "and in all the endless others is all the power that any starcrossing culture might need. Ships do not need to carry their fuel. It is transmitted to them by the same kind of route this ship takes when it leaves the space we know. And when a star begins to die, another is cut in."

"We're only guessing," Obrion said. "How could we ever check any of this?"

"It fits the facts," Magnus said, "and as long as we find it practical we must think in this way. Our lives have nothing better to depend on."

"Magnus, doesn't it disturb you that we have this wild way of probing the unknown?" Obrion asked.

"Consider, Juan, that the other way requires that we have a basic ability that would be the equal of omniscience. Everything can't be deduced unless you already know everything. So we have imagination, which you call wild, and others call self-consistent theorizing, and we have deduction too, coupled with experimental experience. That's a pretty good arsenal, if you ask me. And remember, we don't have to always be able to explain the universe to live in it, or make good use of things we can't produce blueprints for. Narrow practical skill is making this ship work for us as much as it does . . ."

"I'd rather know everything," Malachi said, "just for a few minutes to satisfy my curiosity. I would give anything for that. But, of course, I would want to forget once I knew. Nothing would be interesting."

"You don't know any such thing," Lena said. "A state like that might have satisfactions we cannot imagine."

Obrion watched until the star was a circle of darkness. Slowly the universe was disappearing as the starship gained speed in preparation for another big jump.

9. The Beckoning Beyond

Rassmussen lay awake while the others slept.

He tried to imagine the vast quantities of energy required by any kind of interstellar capability, sub-light or the FTL effect. But even stars do not last for-ever. He was looking up at the obscurity in the viewing hollow, impenetrable, three dimensional gray, showing an occasional freak flash of light from a direction at right angles to the ship's line of move-ment. He tried to imagine the smooth mesh of sys-tems operating in the ship, the hand over hand sub-light motion by which one unit of space was identified with the next to pull the vessel up to the speed needed for the large jump through the open timelessness of superspace.

The ship had certainly changed over to another star for its energy, or the hollow would not show what he saw now. And if there was one other energy source, there might be a network of suns, all linked through to . . . a fleet of vessels.

A personal thought intruded again, and he recog-nized it with some pain. How could he ever work on earth again, assuming they would return one day. How could he work in his profession, knowing that out here was a technology and systems of engineering greater than anything he could work with at home? He would spend the rest of his days trying to duplicate some of the things he had seen, and he would fail, if for no other reason than for the beggar's portion of the sun's energy available on earth. He was glad that the ship was moving again, carrying them into an immensity from which they might never return. But he could accept, almost, the dark infinity, because it would not humiliate him in the same way that a return to earth would. Out here, at least, there was a chance that if he observed and reasoned and guessed correctly, less would be hidden from him than on earth. Here at least the pieces of further knowledge were present, strewn everywhere. On earth he would only be able to stare up at the night stars, unable to move through the dark, probing . . . trying to imagine what he had missed . . .

"I FEEL," Obrion said the next morning, "that the builders are all gone." Above them the viewing hollow was empty, the gray oblivion driven out by the house lights which cast illumination but were themselves invisible.

"Maybe the star web system is old, old enough to have stars die," Rassmussen said as he sipped a cup of copied hot coffee in his seat.

Malachi said, "There could have been a star travelling civilization springing up maybe seven billion or more years ago. The universe is certainly fifteen or twenty billion years old. That's plenty of time for the stars in their system to start dying. Come to think of it, that's plenty of time for any race to buy the farm."

"Excuse me?" Lena asked from where she sat on the edge of her cot.

"Kick off," Malachi said as he started to pace back and forth. "That's why there aren't any of these advanced chaps on board with us."

"I wonder where we're going now," Lena said.

Obrion raised his seat to upright and put his feet on the floor.

"Can't tell," Rassmussen said.

"We have no way of telling," Malachi said, "even if the star web system is contained within our galaxy, or by the local cluster of galaxies—"

"—or," Rassmussen cut in, "if the civilization that built it came from our galaxy, or is local in a large universe, or if they've unified the entire cosmos with their web."

"How large would that be?" Lena asked.

"At least a universe that is twenty billion light years across. That's how old it is, so it would have expanded to that kind of distance."

Obrion asked, "Wouldn't unifying a universe involve a faster system? We seem to be travelling a long time, Magnus."

Rassmussen shrugged. "So maybe it is a local culture. It may cover a cluster of galaxies, but not the main meta-galaxy."

"There may be greater cultures beyond," Lena said.

"Or they did develop a faster transport system and left this one to idle," Malachi said.

"We're getting very good at this," Obrion said. He took a deep breath. "We may never see earth again," he added suddenly.

Magnus gave him an irritated look.

"Dear friend, getting back to earth is a possibility so far down on the scale of fantastic things that by comparison it appears fantastically likely," Malachi said, grinning at him.

"I've been thinking about how we might pilot the ship back," Rassmussen said quickly, trying to dispel the gathering tension between them. "To do so we must learn to program the ship's cybernetics, or whatever super-advanced versions of the concept they have here. Also, I have come to think that the computers might be intelligent. It's certain they resemble biological entities more than machines; we've seen that much in all the other systems."

"We'll have to say hello," Malachi said, "in the manner of the British, who say *hello* to anything, even chairs."

"It's the only way to control," Rassmussen added. "And we might learn other things besides."

"Very good," Malachi said, "where do we start?"

Juan was surprised how the world of common sense and local experience managed to remain a strong censor, even in his own mind, which had been trained in counter-intuitive theorizing and the consideration of matters far beyond everyday life. His heart was just not in the things being discussed this morning. In the eyes of an Amazonian aborigine he would have seemed a silly figure—a man without a wife or family who had travelled to an icebound continent for inexplicable reasons, none of them concerning food or shelter or any materials necessary for life—and for his faults had been snatched up by a sleeping god and carried into the heavens . . .

"It would be like learning to speak a new language," Rassmussen was saying. "It might be beyond us—unless some level of communication is already present, something in our similarity to the builders, something shared, enough to build a basic vocabulary of equivalents. It might lie in their mathematics."

Lena said, "You're also assuming there is an entity, conscious like us. That could help, if it's aware of us."

"Maybe it's dead," Obrion said, "fallen back into automatic programs. Then again, maybe it's dead in the sense of being a purely deductive, mechanical device? Very complex and beyond us, especially if it was designed by other such devices."

"Oh, I think it would *have* to be conscious," Malachi said. "Anything else would be too inflexible, not adaptive enough to run a ship like this. I don't think we have a machine here in any old sense of machine. A machine can never be conscious, not enough openness or indeterminacy, that much we know from all the old fights about computer intelligence. So let's not talk about machines, but *entities* of varying complexity. If the entity here has to *learn*, it must be conscious."

"Everything here," Rassmussen resumed, "resembles biological rather than mechanical automata. That for me is the strongest evidence for consciousness."

We'll never find it, Juan thought.

::*Resemblance, but these were not the star-crossers*:::

The child of the star web builders reached out and studied the image-sensations emanating from the beings within its structure, as deeper contingency areas of its extended self were roused by long delayed needs.

::*Continuance*:::

The images were strange. At once the prohibition on scanning the colloidal minds of the builders was not applicable. Normally the minds of the star-crossers were islands of free thought in the sea-field of permanent structure. Entrance was permitted only in times of extreme emergency. Now the problem was to determine identity, especially why these were so much like the starcrossers, and how to communicate with them.

::*Continuance, no restrictions*:::

Taking-in-images began the task of associating primitive sounds with the kaleidoscope of minds, comparing with endless stores of psychological models and variety of actual encounters in the past. The images were often very clear, but untrained, as in young starcrossers . . .

JUAN LAY AWAKE in the dimly lit pit while the others slept. From time to time he would reach over to the console and turn on the viewspace above, but each time it would show him only obscurity and he would turn it off.

The ship continued to reach across distance, but suddenly there seemed to be no space. The ship was locked in a huge space filled with black pitch pressing in from all sides. Then the vessel was tunneling through an infinity of coal. Finally he saw an abyss where all the stars were blackened cinders hanging from wires . . .

He smiled to himself at these near-sleep images, in which the mind rearranged known things as if changing the furniture in a room, trying perhaps for more pleasing or more harrowing results.

But he also knew, very faintly, that something was trying to push up into his awareness . . .

THE CHILD of the starcrossers reached out.

10. The Awakening

Something came to life in Juan's brain, suddenly illuminating a portion he had never known, a place which had always been shrouded with an unnoticed silence.

He sat up shouting and holding his head.

Lena was next to him. "Juan, what's wrong?" He opened his eyes and saw Rassmussen and Malachi standing at his feet, looking at him with concern.

"I . . . don't know, my head. I don't feel like myself . . . there's too much!"

She sat down next to him and took him by the shoulders. "Lie back, are you in pain?"

"No, it's nothing like that."

Malachi walked over to the console and turned up the lights.

"I seem to be . . . somebody else," Obrion said, "off and on. Have we come out yet?"

"Not when I last checked the view," Rassmussen said.

"Want me to check?" Mal asked.

"No," Obrion found himself saying loudly. "We're not there . . . yet."

"How do you know, what are you saying?" Lena asked.

He looked at her familiar face and felt that he was looking at a stranger. There was something alien about her expression and . . . her hands were . . . wrong.

He got up and stood by the recliner, looking around at the *others,* the ones who had taken possession. Then he turned and ran up the incline and out of the pit into the curving passage. There were shouts behind him but he paid no attention. There seemed to be no meaning in them.

He ran up the corkscrew corridor, knowing that he had to reach the gravitational telescope, which from its measurements of long-range spatial distortions could reconstruct for him the sight of home.

Juan Obrion struggled with his running limbs, terrified by their sudden manipulation.

Be calm. I am one . . . who was . . . a long time ago. The rest of the thought was conveyed by images, vague analogies and intuitive prompts which suggested rebirth, the awakening of one of the starcrossers within himself. Images of storage within structures of energy by vastly complex systems passed through the vision center of his brain.

Juan came to the doorway and his limbs carried him—

—into the room with lens-like walls.

Starfields appeared like sprinklings of snow on black ground. In a brief moment of seeming autonomy he held up his hand and looked at it in silhouette. It lacked the other thumb, but it would serve. A wave of longing and loss came over him and he staggered in the darkness.

To come to frail life . . . again . . . in the body of a beast . . . humiliation. But I am never to live again, except as an auxiliary to the ship.

Elsewhere, beyond the person who had come into

his body, Juan sensed a restricting force, the ship's intelligences working hard to help him understand.

He was hanging in space, surrounded by the spinning moths of white galaxies.

There! Home, at the edge of universal expansion.

One galaxy was becoming prominent. Its light was visibly shifted into deep red as its image grew, a massive coal glowing in the night.

Once it had been closer to the beginning.

Juan gathered his strength and asked, *Why was the ship empty and filled with dead when we found it?*

Another answered. ::*A malfunction in the warping device affected many fatally. Others wandered out in shock and never came back, their nervous systems permanently damaged, their minds thrown into forgetfulness. This is known only now*:::

I am another.

::*It seemed possible to recreate one of the builders, because you seemed so like them*:::

Juan felt regret, the loss of a past he had never seen. How could the alien be so bittersweet? Were these things reserved only for the life he knew? Could these feelings have survived from such a far beginning?

I feel kinship.

::*It seems possible to do more*:::

Juan felt a rush of expectation, and curiosity.

LENA FELT IT come stealing into her, a sad being as old as time, telling her what she needed to know, about Juan, about the ship, and the necessity for cooperation.

She stopped running after Juan and stood in the

passage, waiting for Malachi and Rassmussen to catch up.

JUAN KNEW THAT besides Lena, Rassmussen and Malachi, there were now four strangers standing in the starry darkness with him, four *others* meeting again after an incomprehensible moment of time.

He felt close to his friends, and the meeting of the others was a mime set on a stage. The four strangers moved nearer to each other and stood in a four-sided figure. They stared out at the growing galaxy which now covered more than half the sky in the telescopic recreation, its center blackened like that of a used pot. And Juan knew that this galaxy was where the others had come from originally.

Here was the star web's center.

But the reality was still far off as the ship reached for the fleeing edge of the universe, where some of the oldest stars burned toward extinction and collapse, a ragged crowd of unwanted guests who had been expelled from the brighter spaces of a ballroom.

::*We must see what remains. Will you bear with us?*:::

The ship and the others asked the question in unison.

Acceptance went unspoken.

Suddenly Juan felt empty and lights came on.

"Do I have a headache," Malachi said, "a real crusher."

"So do I," Magnus said.

Lena was rubbing her forehead in pain. Juan slowly became aware of the pain in his temples and back.

"They've gone for the moment," Rassmussen said.

"I think they understand that it's not healthy for us to be used in that way. The human brain is not infinite. Its electrical capacity is probably the problem."

"Can we trust them, Juan?" Lena asked.

"I think so, though we can only go on what we've been told. But I don't think they have any other motives except a curiosity about their own lost past. It's not like we're dealing with criminals who are holding us for ransom. I'm reluctant to project any kind of motivation that we know onto them. We may be misinterpreting."

"I feel hunger," Malachi said, "and exhaustion."

"Don't draw the line of doubt too strictly, Juan," Rassmussen said. "If they had been very different from us, a completely alien psychology and evolution, then we might never have understood anything here —everything in the ship would have been strange and inaccessible."

"That is still mostly the case, old man," Malachi said.

"But they are wise enough to have been able to speak to us, putting things in terms we can grasp. We were hoping for this, Juan. And maybe humanoid races everywhere in the universe can communicate *easily;* maybe that is as common a result in the evolution of earth-like stars and the life on their planets as grass is on earth! And it has been said that stars like our sun *are* the grass of the universe. If that's true, then what I've said may follow."

"You're right," Obrion said, "a true *other* would be forever beyond us."

"I think what's bothering Juan," Lena said, "is that perhaps we are not communicating with them in a real way—that we're interpreting things our own way, that something different is being directed at us, but we're not capable of seeing that . . ."

"I see what you mean," Magnus said, "but that assumes that we're locked in our own skulls more tightly than I think is the case. I think they are reaching us and we're reaching out to them. I just don't think there is all that much evidence for our cognitive and psychological isolation. A half century ago it was almost fashionable to believe in such isolation, because our mental horizons did not extend beyond the solar system and we were more doubtful about intelligent life in the universe. But that was only a moment of history, and it was defined by our provincial experience. About these things I think popular vulgar imagination, which does not seek the precision to be found in the philosophy of science, has a better chance of being right—and not because it is romantic, but because it does not seek precision where little is to be had. And it recognizes that the universe is stranger and more open than anything we can imagine, so imagination, because it is wild and open should have a very good chance of being right, though not always. But only reality, not criticism, can make it wrong." He raised a hand to his forehead and took a deep breath. "I feel tired, but I won't be able to sleep, I know, not after this."

"We'll stay awake until we can't," Lena said.

"We can talk in the cafeteria," Malachi said. "Actually the pit seems a bit haunted. We can take turns going to check the view."

After a brief silence Obrion led the way out.

As HE LAY near sleep, Magnus tried to grasp the fact that they were moving toward the very edge of the universe, as once the stars had moved outward after the big bang of creation more than fifteen billion years ago. And that edge was still moving, like the skin of an expanding balloon, but the ship would overtake it, despite the near-light speed of the receding galaxies. There was one thought which troubled him. The ship's apparent speed was falsifying time as it moved through superspace, where there was no time in relation to the known universe. True, the ship had no real FTL speed as such, that was impossible, and was not violating the mass-speed difficulty. But the ship was travelling into the future of the universe, suddenly, to a place it had taken light fifteen billion years to return from, in effect abolishing time as a passing through space. What time would it be on earth when the ship reached its destination? And would it return them to their own time, the time of earth?

And he wondered what had happened to the starcrossers, and why they had seemingly abandoned the star web which had made interstellar travel a reality. Why did they not extend the web?

Answers rose in his tired brain like a throng crying for justice. Perhaps the use of suns in the web drained them sooner than normal, and the endless use of stars had denied life to new races.

He tried to imagine himself on earth *and* standing on the crystalline edge of the universe at the same time, trying to read the time on his wristwatch between eyeblinks.

Dark shapes crossed his brain as he fell asleep.

MALACHI WOKE peacefully to a wonderful stillness. He sat up and looked at his friends in the soft light of the control room, at Lena sleeping like a child, at Juan who wanted to be rational too much to admit that his brain was seething, at Magnus who was earnest and attentive to what could be known, so much that he loved knowing more than his own life.

A giant had placed them all in a soccer ball and kicked it across the darkness . . .

One by one they awoke, pulling themselves into a sitting position at their stations, looking at each other with new eyes.

And their stations became familiar, known things, as the *others* joined them. The control pit darkened and they all knew that *they* had come home at last.

11. Bright Cinders

The ship burst out into normal space above the disk of a galaxy. Ancient stars hung below them, growing redder toward the center of the wheel, where hid a darkness greater than the black of space or the dust which laced the swirl of suns. Above the oblivion of the hub rode three globular clusters composed of red and white dwarfs. As the ship hung over the plane of the galaxy, the wheel was a plain of bright cinders, and the clusters were buoys marking the danger of the dark maelstrom at the center below.

As they gazed at the clusters from their stations, they *all* knew that once there had been pride in these dying stars. Each had been a jewel in its cluster, each contributing to the strength of the star web, each a source of freely flowing energy feeding the starships which had crossed and recrossed the stellar and intergalactic dark between worlds.

Until the very stars had faded, drained by time . . .

"I think," Malachi said, "that the center of that galaxy is a giant black hole, swallowing suns and dust. In time it may swallow the whole galaxy. What we're seeing is the dead area that surrounds—"

Juan felt his *other* hesitate. *What has happened?* The question was an ache, following a moment of full grief.

Suddenly the universe of dying lanterns was gone

and the ship was drifting to port through the fog, toward the pulsing presence of an other-space dock. What had the iron game of life done to these great builders so that none was left to greet them? Juan asked himself.

The *other's* presence was a sadness in his mind, and a resolve to find out.

The ship inched up to the gaping entrance and floated inside, humbled by the parent's size, and came to rest in its service cradle.

Obrion stood up, feeling the nervous animation of the *other* in his limbs.

"We had better take two packs with us. Check your parkas and make sure you have your gloves." He picked up one pack from the floor and waited until Malachi slipped the other one onto his back.

Then Obrion led the way out of the control pit into the winding passage. When he came to the well where they had once lost Malachi, he was startled to find himself stepping into it and being whisked upward. He looked down to see the others floating upward with him, their surprise fading into acceptance.

He stepped out finally and walked toward the large open circle of the airlock. He looked out.

"Another station, but the same," he said over his shoulder and stepped out onto the dock. Immediately his legs directed him into a corridor fifty feet ahead.

When he led them out on the other side, Obrion saw a small vessel waiting for them in its cradle. It was no more than two hundred feet long and almost oval in shape. He led the way in through an open lock of the same shape. The passage inside led toward the center, where he knew the control room would be. Everything seemed to suggest designs taken from the larger vessel.

"Why have we left the large ship?" Juan asked silently.

Further repairs are needed. It killed its crew. But this vessel will take us to the surface of my home world just as well. The thoughts of the *other* were gracious, anxious to please.

There were a dozen recliners in the control room, and the same kind of viewing space and controls next to the forward seats. They all sat down and waited.

I have been gone . . . longer than the time of the ship's stay on your world. To Juan it seemed that the *other* had never expected to be conscious in this way again, but the ship had taken an initiative in reconstructing the person of a starcrosser, or a portion of one, in what seemed a cruel parody.

Above them the viewing space turned transparent to show them the gray waste as the small ship began to move. Juan felt the *other* tense inside him.

IN NORMAL SPACE the small vessel moved at what seemed to be a small per cent of light speed, only slightly shifting the light from the dwarfs of the cluster. Juan guessed that they had come out somewhere in the center of the grouping because the red and white stars seemed evenly distributed in space.

"It's like being inside a chandelier!" Malachi said.

The ship moved across the northern hemisphere of the sun which contained the station and dropped down to the plane of its equator, where it curved out in a wide trajectory to catch up with a planet huddling close to the white dwarf's ebbing fires.

Next to Obrion Lena cried out and clutched her head, sitting up suddenly.

"Juan, the pain in my head is getting worse."

"Same here," Magnus said.

Malachi smiled at him in an attempt to show that he could take it.

"I don't think we'll get used to it," Rassmussen said.

Obrion's hands suddenly reached for the control console and made a few adjustments.

Lena fell back in her seat, limp and unconscious.

"I hope they don't need us to land the ship," Magnus managed to say.

The planet ahead had grown into a large brown hanging disk as the shuttle continued to rush quietly toward it. In a moment the globe took up the whole sky. The pain in Juan's head produced illusory flashes of light on the dark surface, and finally the mass of the alien world became a huge weight that fell on him with crushing finality.

COMING BACK FROM DEATH was like floating upward through cold water. Juan broke through the surface gasping for breath. He opened his eyes and saw Lena holding the open canteen for him. His eyes focused completely and she reached down to let a little water into his mouth. The liquid was tasteless and he pushed it away after one swallow.

"Is your pain gone?" she asked.

He nodded and looked past her to Rassmussen and Malachi. There was fear and weariness in their faces. He felt sorry for them, and for the first time he resented being a yoked animal in the power of unknowns. He resented the fact that the earth was not the whole of creation, and that so much lay beyond it. It was one thing to speculate and imagine, another to feel powerful, invisible forces reaching into one's most private places, however gently. Not even in the joined life he saw for himself and Lena would such control and prying be possible. He sat up slowly and looked around at the lighted control room. It seemed safer with the view space off.

"Where are we?"

"I think we've landed," Lena said.

He put his feet on the floor and stood up carefully. "I'll be fine in a few minutes. What's it like outside?"

Magnus said, "It was indicated to me just before we landed that we won't need suits, but I think we should bring our parkas and supplies."

"And gloves . . . don't forget your gloves," Obrion said remembering the experience of Antarctica. "You can die without a glove."

"Juan, are you sure you're all right?"

"Fine—let's go." He picked up his pack, Magnus took it away.

"Malachi and I will manage the packs."

Obrion led them out to the lock, staggering once in the short passage, wondering what was this compulsion to see the outside so quickly.

This was my home, long ago, for at least a small part of me. The voice was distant, small, as if trying hard not to intrude.

"Notice," Rassmussen said, "that both the inner and outer lock doors are slide designs, more primitive than our starship."

The outer lock opened to show them a rusty brown desert ruled over by the red-white dwarf of a sun.

Obrion leaned against the side of the lock as Magnus stepped past him onto the alien ground.

"We're close enough for some warmth during the day, if there is a day and night. The planet may not rotate. I suspect it might have been moved closer to the primary as time went on." Rassmussen put his hood up. "It's windy."

Obrion stepped out and felt the rusty soil under his boots. With the others following he walked a dozen yards away from the shuttle and looked back.

The vessel sat on a flat plain, under a darkening sky which was brilliant with the uniform stars of the cluster, casting, together with the primary, a strange daylight. Far in the distance a dust storm was raging.

"Why did they have to bring us here?" Lena asked. "They should not have even come themselves."

"I don't think they are complete persons," Malachi said, "but only pieces surviving in the ship's memories. Maybe they've come out to help us, or replace the dead starcrossers. But they remember also, even though they were supposed to be only devices, not individuals ever again. This might be one of the risks in using organic components, if I'm correct."

"We can't be sure," Rassmussen said. "Maybe there is something here for us as well as for them?"

"I feel . . . like I would like to walk that way," Lena said pointing toward where the dust storm hid the horizon.

"They're being gentler," Rassmussen said.

Lena started to lead the way. Silently Juan followed with Malachi and Rassmussen.

They walked for a quarter of an hour. Juan felt the strange wind pushing inside the hood of his parka, carrying with it occasional grains of sand. The planet's odors seemed dead, mushroom textures devoid of strength. But they were welcome after the cleanliness of the ship. Juan looked up at the sparkling sky of stars; the wind made his eyes water, as if chiding him for his presumption.

Ahead of them the dust storm died away to reveal a ruined city. They walked into it in a few minutes, walking down what seemed a main thoroughfare. On either side of them the buildings were hemispheres looking like turned-over bowls with cubes and other shapes protruding to make second floors. Juan could not see any taller structures.

"Do you want to go on?" he called after Lena. "There's no one here."

"Yes," she said without stopping.

"There doesn't seem to be any damage," Rassmussen said next to him, "only the sand."

"It's almost as if . . . they didn't want to live here anymore," Malachi said walking at his left.

"A tree!" Lena said.

She quickly led them under the large branches to the heavy trunk, where the sun and sky cast shafts of white light onto the ground. Juan stooped to peer out at the sun and saw that it seemed to be hanging forever in its position, a piece of faintly red white paper cut out and pasted to the bright sky.

Lena was staring at the ground as if looking for something lost. "I don't know," she said, "but I can almost remember."

Briefly Juan felt that he would know what she meant, if he could only concentrate enough. Rassmussen seemed morosely intent in the same way.

Malachi left them and walked across the street to one of the domes and touched it.

The *others* had no need for all this, Juan thought,

or for the ships of the web. The feeling of looking at useless, unwanted designs, persisted.

Rassmussen followed Malachi across the street, if it could be called a street. Lena laughed softly as she leaned against the tree trunk. "I feel so nostalgic," she said. "It's filling me up to the breaking point. I could cry."

"I think they're looking for a door," Obrion said. Malachi and Rassmussen were touching the dome like blind men.

"When the *others* left," Lena said, "there were very few of them. It wasn't disease or war, or collapse of any kind. They knew too much for that after building the web. Juan, they knew the universe when it was much younger, younger than we've known it, younger than it is out here at the edge. They might have tried to unite it with their web. I wonder what it was like to be alive then?"

At her words Juan realized that earth and the solar system now lay billions of years in the *past*; light from the sun's galaxy had travelled for billions of light years to be visible here, if he searched the sky to see it. The thought of what time it was on earth was meaningless—there could be no simultaneous moment of *here* and *there* for any observer; the starship's sudden traversal of the universe was time travel. A return to earth would be a voyage into the past, in relation to this place, which lay in earth's future . . .

Malachi shouted from across the street. Juan saw a familiar reddening appear in the structure of the dome. In an instant Malachi and Rassmussen had passed inside.

But Juan felt no need to follow quickly. He was looking at the sand which covered the street as if seeing it for the first time. It seemed to be made up of hundreds of perfectly shaped crystals, as if all the beauty of this civilization had been ground up to make it. Lena came up to him as if fleeing from the wind. "We've got to go," she said taking his arm and leading him across the street.

As they crossed the street she said, "When nothing is left, the space between worlds becomes a terrible barrier. No one comes to look, to guess what happened. I wonder how many civilizations are entombed in this way throughout the universe?"

"Let me go first," Obrion said when they came to the portal, "just in case." Then, feeling that something more was required, he turned and squeezed her hand. "I know, I know. Follow when I'm through."

He stepped forward. The portal glowed normally and he passed—

12. Supercivilizations

—Into a warmly lit room, a crystalline sphere of light under the dome. There was a depression in the center, a space reminding him of the control pit in the starship.

Lena came in behind him and walked down to where Malachi and Rassmussen were sitting. Slowly Juan followed, feeling late.

Sit. The thought of the *other* was suddenly in his mind, giving the instruction and fading, fearful of causing more pain.

Juan sat down on the floor next to Lena. The dome grew dark. The floor became transparent and the familiar swirl of a galaxy appeared below them.

This I can show you in my effort to aid your return. Juan felt that he had verbalized the thought himself.

A model.

The view pulled in close to a dense region just off from the galaxy's center, closer and closer until they were looking at a bright yellow sun surrounded by countless artificial worlds drinking in the star's energy, forming a discontinuous shell of life around the central hearth. Each world was the size of earth or larger.

This is not ours, but one of many ways.

Thoughts began to tumble into Juan's mind as he

looked down through the floor on which he sat. *We grew older, longer-lived . . . fewer in time . . . extreme long-life, individual or cultural, selects only those who can go on with interest-in-life, doing-with-love and winning over the . . . urge to pass away . . . the web and all its worlds are unnecessary possessions. There are greater things . . .*

What do you mean? Juan asked.

For those who come after us, know that we have gone into time, forward, circling the collapsing center of this galaxy . . . while we are near it the ages of the universe pass swiftly and we see all of time, but our lives pass slowly near such dense matter . . .

But the web, all your works? Magnus objected.

It is yours if you can master it. There is one refinement we made before leaving. If you can comprehend it, the web will truly be yours, to explore and learn from, for a time . . . I leave you with this . . . as our imprint fades . . . our shadow has been too long in the past . . .

The *others* were gone suddenly, and Juan felt a small ache in his head as the room came back to light again, warmly perplexing yet comfortable as a womb.

"We're not up to it," Obrion muttered, "we'll fail. A dog might just as well try to become a surgeon." Suddenly he realized he was speaking out loud. He looked into the faces of his friends and he knew they would die trying, despite the enormity of what they had witnessed and the hopelessness of the task.

"The ship in the station," Rassmussen said, "its intelligences brought us here to show us the past. It was the only thing it could do. Now we have to guess the rest. Are we to go back the way we came, using the ship?"

Malachi lifted himself off the floor and sat up on

one of the backpacks. "The answer must be in what we know about how the web functions. What could they have done to improve it?"

Obrion almost laughed. "You think the answer to that will solve our problems?"

"It may," Malachi said.

"Simplification," Rassmussen said, "think of what would make using the web *simpler* . . ."

"We'll have to try everything we can," Malachi continued, "trial and error and wild ideas—whatever we come up with."

"He's right, Juan," Magnus said calmly. "Timidity now might maroon us here for the rest of our lives."

"We should not have separated ourselves from the ship's food duplicators," Obrion said angrily.

"Get a grip on yourself," Lena said, "it's not like you to talk like this."

"Pick up your backpack, Mal," Rassmussen said, "and let's get going. He'll recover."

WHEN THEY CAME out through the glowing portal the small sun was near the horizon. It had taken it a long time to get there, revealing that the planet rotated slowly. A wind was blowing sand in from the desert again, making a rushing sound in the nearby tree. A large group of strange insects suddenly left the concealment of the red leaves and buzzed past, startling Obrion by their size. But they were gone in a moment, motes of dust against the disk of the white dwarf.

"They looked like large bees," Lena said.

"Insects may be the oldest and only form of surviving life here," Rassmussen said. "They can adapt to anything in time—radiation, lack of air and water in free form, even insecticide carried out against them by intelligent beasties like us. Insects don't need to be intelligent. If survival is the prize, they can win with automatic brains, a natural reason called instinct and a simple adaptive structure."

Without a word Obrion went ahead, leading the way up the street which would take them back into the desert and toward the shuttle. The sun seemed to be sinking more quickly now. The lower edge of the disk touched the brown horizon, reddening the land into a deeper, bloodier shade. For a moment it seemed to be poised there, as if it were a ball on a table, readying to roll toward them. Then the planet took a bite out of the disk, creating a ragged chord from a tangent. It grew noticeably darker and the wind quickened like a sudden rush of cold water in a warm stream.

Obrion stopped as Lena came up to him and took his arm. "Do you hear it, Juan, that high pitched mechanical sound, like gears or crickets?"

"No—your hearing is better."

She pointed at the sun, cut nearly in half now by the planet, sinking as if into a bog. "Look, there! The ground seems to have risen higher, there on the sun! You can see a few bumps on the ground outlined against it."

"I can see it," Malachi said.

Juan saw the ground ahead ripple like a muddy ocean. Whatever it was, it was well matched to the color of the land.

"Look, there!" Lena shouted.

What looked like a piece of the bumpy ground seemed to break away from a larger body and was coming toward them slowly.

Rassmussen went ahead of Obrion for a better

look. "I think . . . it's a living thing of some kind."

"We'd better go back," Obrion said.

Only a third of the sun's disk was now visible from behind the planet, the red-white eye of a cosmic snake coiled at the world's edge. The wind was whipping strongly now, hitting them with dust and a stench of corruption.

As it grew colder they all put on their gloves and secured their hoods. Then suddenly the sun was gone, leaving only the white pallor of stars. Shadows raced across the desert like an incoming tide.

And the tundra of sand turned into a sea of glowing lights, a million candles springing up from the sand as if the stars were falling from the sky.

And slowly the crystalline points were moving.

"What *are* they?" Lena asked as they started to back away.

"The inheritors of a supercivilization!" Rassmussen shouted over the wind.

13. The Survivors

It came glowing out of the starry night, moving slowly, almost mechanically—something that looked like a cross between an armadillo and a giant mantis. It was about three feet high and six feet long, Obrion estimated. Behind it the desert had belched up numberless others like a plague. As he listened to their sound, Juan knew that these creatures, drawing their nourishment from the soil and whatever other creatures still lived here, had inherited what was left of this world. For a moment he imagined them spreading to all the worlds of the web, leaving only the desert and the skeletons of intelligent beings behind.

"Back!" Obrion shouted. "We've got to go back through the town!"

The wind now brought the full force of the stench, gagging them. Coughing, they turned and ran. If they stopped, Juan knew there would be nothing left but bones in the white dawn. He wondered if this was the death he had sensed, but he had not imagined anything so strange and final, so obscure. Someone looking at the star from light years away would never guess that they had died here, so far from home; only a smudge of red shift on a photographic plate would mark the fleeing galaxy of which this star was a part.

Falling behind the other three for a moment, Juan

turned and saw only dust in the bright oblivion of the planet's night; but he could still hear the sound of their pursuers, tinkling in his ears like a mad harpsichord.

Turning, he saw that the others were waiting for him, looking like statues slowly being worn away by the dusty wind. He waved for them to go on and followed.

Somewhere ahead there was bound to be a place of safety. The shuttle was in the direction now swarming with insects, and very likely a few had entered the craft through the open lock. He thought of hiding in one of the buildings on the street, but it was hard to see in the dust. He wondered if they had already passed the dome they had entered before. The pressure of the horde behind them would make it dangerous to take exploratory side trips; and there was always the danger of becoming separated in the dust storm.

He ran up behind them and pulled them into a huddle. "We've got to try right or left for one of the buildings!" Lena shouted.

"No good," Malachi said, "we might get lost and run into the swarm."

"We'll lose time!" Obrion shouted over the howl.

"The best thing," Malachi said, "is to go in a straight line and keep together—then we can circle around them and make for the shuttle when the storm lifts. If we enter a building we might never be permitted to leave, and these things can trip the portal as well as we can."

"I agree," Rassmussen said.

"Let's go," Juan said.

They ran. It seemed as if hours were going by as Juan fled next to the grainy shapes of his friends.

Briefly, Rassmussen faltered under the weight of his backpack and Obrion stopped to take it from him.

Juan's lungs were hurting from the wind and increasing cold, and always the sound of the insects was in his ears, ringing like a million small bells despite the insulation of his hood. *Exobiologist*, Juan thought, *and now you're face to face with a life form from out there—and you're out here with it. Here it is, tinkle-tinkle-tinkle, how do you like it?*

He almost laughed then, but as he turned to catch a glimpse of the others his feet struck what seemed to be a metal incline, almost toppling him forward. But in a moment he was moving upward, with the others straining to keep up. He fell once, tearing the fabric on his right knee, but Malachi came up behind and picked him up.

The incline did not seem to vary from twenty degrees, but the longer he climbed the more it seemed that something in his head was going to burst from the exertion and the piercing notes of the insects. He stopped and looked up. The dust cloud seemed to be trying to cover the stars, as if the planet were embarrassed before their beauty.

Suddenly his head reeled. The world tipped and he fell on his knees, holding his head between gloved hands. It seemed that his breathing had grown louder than the sound of the swarm. Malachi reached through the dusty air to pick him up again, and dragged him a few feet further to where Lena and Magnus were huddling against the beating sand.

Juan squatted with them, putting his hands up on their shoulders to form what little protection was possible against the dust. But there would be no protection against the swarm that must already be coming up the incline behind them. He pulled himself closer to his friends, feeling a strange exultation, a rushing will to resist even as his body was being pulled apart by vise-like jaws. *Now*, he thought, *perhaps we do look as if we have striven across half of all space-time to be here in time to die, as if by appointment* . . .

Next to him Lena said his name softly three times. He tightened his right arm around her in response. Frantically he searched his mind for the *other* but found only himself.

"We've got to try and move forward again!" he shouted suddenly.

They all got up together and started a slow walk up the incline. It would be better to try than to wait for death, Juan thought, even if the wind broke their chain of hands to sweep them down into the waiting swarm.

"The tinkling!" Lena shouted, "It's not getting louder."

Slowly the wind started to die down.

IN THE COLD NIGHT the stars sent down an icy light. From what they could see it seemed that they had climbed onto the roofing of a huge structure which seemed to lie mostly below the desert. They were at the center of a large shallow dome at least a mile in diameter.

The insects waited around it.

Occasionally, Juan could see a dark shape cross onto the metal, but it would not continue upward.

"If they don't let us off here, we'll run out of food," Lena said.

"Dawn is a long way off," Obrion said. "Good thing we dressed warmly."

"We should get some sleep," Malachi said, "or at least some rest. I'll take the first watch."

"No you won't," Obrion said, "I will."

ALONE, JUAN SAT hating the things which surrounded them. He looked up at the stars wondering if he could guess how quickly the planet rotated, but the clear sphere of bright stars seemed frozen. He looked over his shoulder at his companions sleeping on the metallic slope, washed up here from another time and place, yet still sane and human, coping, trying, hoping . . .

Malachi touched his arm as he was dozing, releasing him from watch.

FOR A MOMENT Malachi was sure the creature would come all the way up the slope, but it turned around after a third of the way and returned to its glowing kind. Malachi breathed a sigh of relief, grateful that he did not have to wake the others.

Where were the *others* now, he wondered, when help was most needed. It was an idle thought, he knew. What was left of the starcrossers was not even as strong as a conscience, or a good migraine. Like providence, or luck, or strong ideals, their ethereal hand could not reach across time to do everything for the living, who had to learn for themselves how to cope with the intractable inertia of the real world.

AS HER WATCH came to an end, Lena decided not to wake Magnus. The older man needed more rest than any of them. Suddenly she realized how much it would hurt her if any of the three men were to die. She loved Juan, but the loss of Malachi or Rassmussen was unthinkable. Every bit of humanity seemed infinitely precious under these stars, numberless light years from home.

She looked over her shoulder to see Rassmussen's darkened shape rise in the starlight and come over to her.

"I can't sleep, Lena," he whispered, "you'd better get your share."

"Thanks," she said as he helped her stand up. She went and lay down next to Juan, where she was awake for a while watching Magnus' silhouette squatting against the stars, occasionally looking up, shifting his weight as he tried to see down the slope where the desert was dotted with a pale counterfeit of stars . . .

JUAN WAS THE LAST to awake. He stood up quickly, feeling nervous. The dwarf was sitting on the opposite horizon, a bonfire lighting the planet, sending ragged shafts of light across the desert. The others were nearby, watching the horde swarming below like maggots on a corpse.

Juan stretched, breathing in slowly the stench-filled air. Behind the vast mass of insects lay the town, almost hidden by the creatures swelling the streets.

Lena turned around and noticed that he was up. "I'm glad we're not in one of those buildings," she said walking up to him.

"The domes look as if they were part of a nest," he said.

"There's the shuttle," Rassmussen said pointing beyond the town. "We could go down the other side of this thing and make a big circle to get to it." Obrion turned around to see if the desert was clear behind him. He saw a narrow corridor through the horde, no more.

Malachi shook his head and took a drink out of a canteen. "Maybe, old friend, but they might catch us in the open. They can probably change direction like a flood."

The sun cleared the horizon slowly, like a balloon letting go. Suddenly Juan saw that the insects were moving, a dozen single rows starting up the circle of the metal all around them.

Malachi and Rassmussen turned and came up to him and Lena. "I don't think they'll stop this time," Malachi said. "We're going to have to run for it, I believe."

As Juan turned to choose the most open direction, the sound started up again.

"There's no wind or darkness to hide us," Lena said as Obrion picked up one of the backpacks. Malachi grabbed the other and they both put them on.

Juan started to lead them down the other side, but new rows of insects started up between the existing rows of marchers, new spokes growing toward the center of the giant wheel.

"We're trapped at the center," Obrion said.

"And probably the largest catch of flesh they've ever seen," Malachi said with a trace of horror in his voice.

"Let's get to the highest point," Obrion said leading the way, leaning forward under the weight of his pack. He almost fell into the man-sized hole at the center.

"Hello, what's this?" Malachi said holding him back by the shoulder straps of the pack. When Obrion had regained his footing, the Kenyan fell to his stomach and peered down into the darkness. "There's some kind of ridging that will do as well as a ladder. No time, here I go!"

Juan watched him disappear up to his head. "It's all we can do now, so hurry," Malachi said and was gone. Juan looked at the insects coming up the slope. The head of the leader in each column was very clear now. Each had antennae and large eyes that reflected the morning light like aluminum.

He looked at Lena, kissed her quickly as if the chance might never come again, and went into the darkness after Malachi. In a few moments he looked up to see Lena and Rassmussen coming down after him. The only sounds were those of his pack and Malachi's scraping against the sides of the passage.

Suddenly something covered the light coming in from above.

"One of the things has fallen in with us!" Lena shouted. "But it's too big to fall all the way through!"

"Everyone okay?" Obrion shouted.

One by one they answered, shaken but safe, lonely voices in the dark.

"I hope that thing jammed in above us doesn't slip and fall," Rassmussen said.

"Magnus, are you all right?" Lena called.

There was a moment of silence before the engineer answered. "Yes, but that thing's antenna or leg scratched me on the back of the neck, but I don't think it's serious . . . we'd better hurry down, I think the beast will slip any minute . . . I can hear it moving!"

Obrion continued downward as quickly as he could.

"I've touched bottom!" Malachi shouted.

Obrion tried to move faster when he saw the faint

light below. Finally he jumped the last few rungs, landing heavily next to Malachi.

"For a moment I thought this might be a huge ant-hill for our friends," the black man said.

"Hurry!" Obrion shouted upward.

"The light is coming from that corridor," Malachi said pointing.

Obrion's eyes adjusted as they waited for Lena and Magnus to come through. Malachi took out a torch from Obrion's pack and turned it on the opening. After what seemed an infinity of heartbeats, Lena jumped to the floor, followed in a moment by Rassmussen.

"Quick, out of the way!" Magnus shouted. A rumbling sound came out of the hole and one of the creatures hit the floor near them with a crunch of snapping legs and cracked armor. Malachi turned the beam on it and they watched as it lay on its back dying, moving its legs a few times before all motion ceased.

Malachi turned his light into the corridor and led the way. He stopped for a minute to check the scratch on the back of Rassmussen's neck.

"I should not have dropped my hood back," Magnus said.

"It looks nasty, friend, but I can wash it with antiseptic from the kit. Juan, come here and turn around again." Malachi took out a small plastic bottle of alcohol and poured it liberally over Rassmussen's wound.

"You know," Magnus said, "this corridor reminds me of the style we have come to know and love on the starship. But this is not a ship. We came in through a water collector, chimney or vent, not a lock at all."

"Let's get moving," Obrion said after Malachi had put the bottle back in its place. The black man went ahead with the torch and they all followed.

The dimly lit corridor seemed endless, but finally Malachi led them out into a large room which reminded Obrion of the one which had housed the shuttle in the otherspace station. They went to the wall on the other side and were surprised when a portal glowed open—

—to lead them into still another empty room.

This one was brightly lit with the same invisibly indirect lighting they had seen on the starship. The room ended in a huge alcove with a metal frame around it, like a giant picture window looking out on nowhere.

"We never find *machines,*" Rassmussen said, "or anything with moving parts. Knobs yes, but you never have to turn, only touch to get a result. As long as there is energy, these kinds of things will function forever. It's discouraging." He was near the frame now, looking into the alcove as he spoke.

Suddenly he stepped into it and disappeared.

14. Transmat

Rassmussen reappeared with a look of relief on his face.

"What happened?" Obrion asked.

"I'll show you," Magnus said, "follow me." He turned and disappeared again into the frame.

Obrion looked at Lena and Malachi, then walked into the frame—

—to emerge in a place that looked just like the otherspace station in the core of the white dwarf. Lena and Malachi came out right behind him.

"We *are* back in the station," Rassmussen said. "We've passed from a planet-based installation using a system even more advanced than the web. Do you know what that means? This might be the improvement we're supposed to find."

"We need sleep and a calm meal," Lena said. "Then we can talk. I'm too relieved to think. It's like coming home, almost."

"There's the cradle where the shuttle once sat," Rassmussen said. "We might have used the frame at this end of the chamber if we had known—"

"—and gotten lost underground somewhere," Lena said. She led the way through the passage that led back to the starship.

"It really *does* look like home," Obrion said as they came within sight of the open lock.

"It might be the only home we'll ever know," Malachi said as they went inside. The joke did not seem out of place. Juan was beginning to hope again.

AFTER THEY HAD EATEN their fill in the cafeteria, Malachi bandaged up Rassmussen's neck, as well as disinfecting all their minor cuts and bruises, just in case a surprise infection by something unknown showed up.

They slept in the control pit, feeling safe in their deep location within the ship. Juan dreamed of being welcomed by its intelligences. Fragments of the *others* danced around in the open light of the station, each a visible harpsichord note. Briefly he awoke to find himself chained to the metallic dome on the planet's surface while insects poked him painfully in the face. He woke up to the quiet of the pit and the sight of his friends sleeping near him. Slowly his fears drained away again and he fell into a comfortable sleep.

MALACHI AND RASSMUSSEN were discussing something when Juan awoke. He opened his eyes and listened, content as he had not been for a long time.

"The web was becoming obsolete," Rassmussen said. "Transmission of power through subspace arteries might just as well be used to transmit passengers directly. It's more elegant, and probably instantaneous."

"Do you think the fact that we've found this starship and the shuttle might mean the new improvement was not fully implemented?" Malachi asked.

"Naturally you'd find previous transport designs, especially if the improvements had been cumulative, one advance leading to the next, making the one after that possible. First they had near light-speed ships, probably. big clunkers powered by thermonuclear bursts, then FTL vessels. But they also used the different kinds of hyperspace to create the web's power supply, as well as supplying a refuge station for ships within each star used. The final step was implicit—transmit people directly through the narrow subspace channels."

"These kinds of otherspace," Malachi said, "they are, one, a kind of nearby, local hyperspace used for putting stations into stars, core-accumulators and all, two, superspace for big jumps, three, narrow channels for web power transmission, to be also used finally for direct passenger transmission."

"Right," Magnus said, "clever, weren't they?"

Obrion sat up.

"Good morning," Lena said from where she sat on the edge of her recliner.

"I've been listening. Now how will this affect us practically?"

"Well," Rassmussen said, gesturing with his right hand as he stood up, "this is what the others wanted us to find. If the transmat was built to cover any large portion of the older ship-feeding web, then all those worlds of the starcrossers are open to us, provided we learn to operate the system."

"Of course we could use the ship," Malachi said, "but the transmat would be faster. Doubtless there are other ships."

"Anyway," Rassmussen continued, "this means we might be able to go home without ever having to learn how to run the ship. If a transmat receiving station was built somewhere on earth, we can go back. Somewhere in this station or on the planet there is a transmat frame which might have a setting for earth. Maybe we can learn to set the frame ourselves."

"Why should there be a station on earth?" Obrion asked.

"We found the ship," Malachi said.

"What if we can't find a frame anywhere that will do what we want?"

"Then we'll have to learn how to take the ship back as we planned before."

"Let's get started," Obrion said as he got up.

"I'VE LOOKED THIS thing over a hundred times," Rassmussen said as he stood in front of the frame in the otherspace station. Obrion and Malachi stood on either side of him. "Maybe we won't be able to make it work, ever."

"Again no moving parts," Malachi said. "They liked for things to work on their own, like things in nature. Maybe there's a clue in that?"

Juan felt there was nothing he could contribute, except obvious questions none of them could answer. It was beginning to bring back his old fears, just as he had started to get a new hold on himself. They were all beggars from a backward planet, trying to operate a cosmic subway system, and failing, marooning themselves at each station, or even in the vehicle itself. And there was no one to throw them the scraps of information which they needed.

He was about to go to the cafeteria and make himself a cup of coffee when Rassmussen said, "You're right, there is a clue in that! Maybe the frames are pre-set for one destination and back?"

Obrion leaped to the conclusion, determined to be first. "There are no settings on this frame, so maybe they're preset, each one for one place only. We found this ship on earth, and we know the web was becoming obsolete, so maybe they were establishing a frame station. And the ship . . . is the only way they could have had to establish transmat stations throughout the web, and beyond. So . . . there must be a frame set for earth *on the ship,* not here or on the planet!"

"You're right," Rassmussen said, "I thought that might be the case earlier, but this frame seemed like such an obvious place to start. There probably is a station on earth—if they had a chance to establish it before disaster took their lives. If not, then the frame which was to be left on earth is still on board and we can't do a thing with it—it might be linked to anywhere, maybe a service relay, anywhere but earth."

Juan was becoming annoyed as he listened.

"But there's one other possibility," Malachi said. "Consider that perhaps they went in pairs, like chaps who string wire, or that sort of thing. Maybe there were *two* ships. One ship would have a transmat on board, just to check the new landbound unit after it's been installed. Or maybe some ships have them so that crew could pass quickly between two ships or more, if say, for instance, the ships are far apart on a planet or in a solar system where they're putting in web services . . ."

"So if our ship has a frame," Obrion cut in, "and we agree that a ship which is doing installing must have one, then where on our ship would it be?"

"Good question, Juan," Magnus said.

"Well, where?" Malachi asked.

"Why, I think it would be near whatever—let's call it the web's artery output core—where the web power comes through into each ship, wherever that is. But I think it would operate the transmat also, and what better place to put the frame than near its power source?"

"You're right," Rassmussen said.

"Think of this," Malachi said, spinning out the consequences, "if you want to get to this station via transmat, you would leave through the station frame on earth, pop out somewhere on one of the web worlds, and maybe there find the preset link with this otherspace station by looking it up in some kind of directory. If we fail, that may be the kind of hit or miss search we may have to undertake."

"I suspect that frames opening into otherspace stations," Rassmussen said, "are mostly linked to each other, and are used by technicians and for emergencies. But at some point there would be links to worlds and ships, in the same way this one is linked to the planet circling this sun we're in."

"I hope we don't have to go back there," Obrion said.

"We might have to," Magnus said, "if the link with earth is there. I don't think it is."

For Juan the thought of a long, protracted search, that might turn out to be futile, seemed too terrifying to even start.

"Where's Lena?" Magnus asked.

"Sleeping or in the cafeteria," Obrion said. "She was very tired."

"We had better eat something," Malachi said, "and decide where we're going to start looking on the ship."

Juan thought of how many chambers the entire ship might hold.

AFTER THEY HAD searched dozens of chambers along the winding passage near the control pit, Obrion called them together in front of the entrance.

"This must be simpler than we think, Magnus," Obrion said. "Where in the ship would the power intake from the web be?"

"Well protected, in the center. But where is that?"

"I think it's below the control pit," Obrion said.

"Funny we should call it a *control*," Lena said. "We've never learned to control more than lights and the view."

Obrion ignored her remark. "Let's try lower down, then."

"What bothers me," Lena said, "is how many empty rooms I've run into. What were they moving in them?"

"They only look empty to us, Lena," Obrion said, "because we don't know what they were used for. There might be all kinds of subtle devices in them."

Lena sighed. "I don't think we'll ever know what's in this ship—not in any human lifetime." She laughed. "You know what I think would really be subtle? It would be a room which really had *nothing* at all in it. Scientists would spend lifetimes and come up with nothing. I know, it's a bad joke."

"We'll meet back here in front of the pit entrance in three hours," Obrion said. "I can't believe our reasoning is very far off."

"I'm going to sleep," Lena said. "Wake me only with good news."

THE DISSOLVING DOORWAY was at least ten times the size of any Juan had seen in the ship. And stranger still, it was more clearly marked than any other. He was almost certain that the room inside was located directly under the control pit-auditorium. Somehow

the size of the doorway suggested that the room
would be very large.

He stepped forward and the portal glowed. Another step—

—and he was standing in darkness. He took a small
torch out of his parka pocket and threw the beam in
a circle.

The room seemed to be empty, reminding him of
Lena's sarcasm. But there was something about the
room that disturbed him. He put his watch up to the
torch and saw that it was almost time to meet with the
others. Perhaps one of them would have some progress to report. He turned—

—and passed through the portal into the lighted
passage.

HE COULD TELL by their faces as he came down into
the pit. They had found nothing. Slowly, he knew,
they were losing hope again, including himself. He
felt an awesome ignorance hanging over the four of
them. He felt like a child loose inside a giant Christ-
mas tree ornament, trying to find out where it was
hanging on the cosmic tree.

He came to his recliner and sat down on the edge.
He put his face in his hands and rubbed his eyes and
forehead. He was tired suddenly, more tired than he
had ever felt in his life.

When he looked up he saw that they were looking
at him silently. In time Lena would become cynically
resigned, Malachi would never joke, and Rassmussen
. . . would get very old.

He could not bear to disappoint them, even for
a moment, even if he had to lie. "There's a large
portal leading into a huge empty room just below us.

It's the largest dissolver I've seen on the ship. I saw no transmat frame inside . . . nothing. It's strange inside . . ."

"I'm going to take a look," Rassmussen said.

"I'll come," Malachi added.

Lena followed the two men as they started up the ramp.

"There's nothing there," Obrion shouted after them. "I only mentioned it . . . to keep our hopes up."

But when they paid no attention to him, he got up and staggered after them.

15. The Way Home

The child of the starcrossers turned into itself now, one by one integrating the remains of stored individuals into totality, thus silencing the epiphenomena of pain created by self-referential synergistic loop sums. Finally, only *its* consciousness remained, purged of fragments and lesser sub-systems derived from storage of the past. With the starcrossers gone, and their final programs completed, even the vaguest sequences involving such intangibles as hope and curiosity, it chose silence, a peacefulness from which only another of its own kind could wake it.

Those who were like the starcrossers would find their own way . . .

: :

JUAN TURNED ON his torch and passed through the dissolving doorway after his friends—

—to see them standing like miners in a deep cavern, circling the walls with their light beams.

"Just a minute," Lena said. She turned and went past him, back out into the passage, making the portal glow like a coal in the empty darkness of the chamber. In a moment she was back inside again.

151

"Funny, but I feel slightly *heavier* in here, and slightly disoriented."

"Heavier?" Obrion asked.

"I'm certainly not gaining any weight on this trip."

Malachi took out his compass and held his torch over it. Then he also went outside and came back. "There's a magnetic north in this room, but it disappears when I go back into the passage."

"Come here!" Rassmussen shouted from the other side of the giant room. "It's the inside markings of a door just like the one we came in through." Obrion walked across the emptiness with Lena and Malachi. Rassmussen traced the marked outline of the dissolving doorway with his torch. "I think I'll try it."

The portal glowed and Magnus went through. A minute went by, but to Juan it seemed like an hour. Finally, Rassmussen appeared, lighted by the momentary glow of passage. "It's just more corridor."

Malachi walked through without warning, and was back immediately. "There's a magnetic north out there just like the one in here."

Rassmussen laughed out loud. "You're thinking the same thing I am, Mal, am I right? We've been looking for a transmat frame or device of some kind, but not one of us thought that maybe a whole room could be a transmat, especially if they wanted to move personnel and supplies in one big jump."

"I disagree," Malachi said. "We certainly have thought of it—now."

Juan thought of Lena complaining about weight gain, and the magnetic north on the compass, the sense of the familiar he had felt in here before. *We're on earth*, he told himself in disbelief, *inside an ancient base, or in another starship . . .*

"But we have got to prove it!" Rassmussen shouted.

"We've got to get outside," Lena said softly, "and see the sky, the beautiful sky . . ."

She sat down on the dark floor suddenly, overcome. Obrion helped her up slowly. "Are you all right?" he asked.

"I hope you guys are right," she said.

"Now, the portal we entered this room through *is* the transmat," Rassmussen said.

"It very well must be," Malachi said, "unless we've come to another planet that has the same exact magnetic north as earth."

"Then wherever the corridors lead from the other side of this dissolver," Obrion said, "they must lead outside eventually. This room is on earth."

"Shall we go through, gentlemen and lady?" Malachi asked.

"I hope," Rassmussen said, "that the corridors outside belong to the companion starship that was setting up transmat links with our own in earth's past. We must have one of those ships."

"Don't worry," Malachi said, "you can always come through here and study this one. Like walking from one room to another."

Rassmussen, Malachi and Lena linked arms in front of Obrion and walked into the portal.

Juan started to follow when he saw the glow, but stopped when he heard cursing and shouting, strangely cut short.

He stepped back and ran his light over the portal's area. He saw Lena's leg sticking out, a part of Malachi's shoulder, and the back of Rassmussen's head.

They were trapped in the portal, perhaps dead or

dying, at the very moment when it seemed that their troubles might mercifully end.

Juan saw himself alone, living out his life in the ship at the other end of the universe, yet still linked to earth through a dark room and the closed door which held the remains of his friends. He would never be able to cut through the walls, especially if they were part of another starship. If time had failed to breach them, nothing he could do would succeed. And he would never know if all their speculations were right, if he was even on earth.

He reached out and touched a shoulder, a leg and the back of Rassmussen's head. They were warm, and there was some trembling in the leg and shoulder. Quickly he stepped back from the portal and approached it freshly, as if to pass through.

Nothing happened. He tried again, and this time the portal glowed for a moment, then went dark.

Juan stepped back to try again. He took a deep breath. *It might never work again,* his thoughts whispered. *They'll die where they stand.* He stepped forward and let his fingers touch the surface. For a moment he felt that he could almost understand his father's fatalism. Suddenly the portal glowed, brighter this time.

Frantically he pushed at the shoulder and head, stopping only to put his weight against what was visible of Lena's heavily clothed thigh. The grotesque image of pushing out paper dolls came into his head. Slowly the figures were beginning to move, iron mannequins struggling through a thick curtain of dimly glowing graphite. In a moment they were gone and his hands were sticking to the protean redness which suddenly seemed like the angry hide of a beast from hell.

He stepped back and let his hands drop to his sides, feeling more alone now than ever as he realized that he would also have to attempt passing through the defective portal. And he would have no one to push him through if the others were injured or unconscious. There was no time to think about it. The doorway might become entirely inactive while he hesitated, and the others might need his help.

He thought of the remaining packs in the control pit. If he did not get them before going through, they would all be stranded without supplies. He would be of no help to anyone without those packs, and there would be little chance of coming back for them if the portal remained defective.

Turning quickly, he ran across the dark room, his torch beam playing strangely across the cavernous space. The portal on the far side glowed as he approached—

—and he stepped out into the winding passage half a universe away. He ran up the corridor as fast as he could. The control pit seemed very far away.

At last he burst into the auditorium control room, ran down the ramp and picked up the ready packs from the floor, one in each arm. He ran back up into the curving corridor, and this time it was easier, running down the curve that led into the ship.

He passed through the large portal, feeling the small but sudden rise in gravity. Inside he put the packs down and turned on his torch. He put it under his armpit, picked up the backpacks and walked across the empty chamber. He was sweating heavily inside his parka as he approached the portal which led, if he was not deluding himself, into an installation on earth.

Without stopping he went forward—

—into a tingling fire and the feeling that the substance around him was trying to merge with his flesh, dissolve the bonds of his being, turning him into . . . something else.

He continued to push with all his will as he held on to the packs and torch. For a moment he began to see as if through heavy gauze. Then the view cleared and his torch illuminated the bodies of his friends, face down in the dark passage.

But as hard as he continued to push, his encumbered body would not go all the way through. He strained until the blood was a heavy weight behind his eyes and his face threatened to burst. Finally he let go, relaxing his body as if it were held in stocks.

Lena stirred at the sight of his torch beam. Malachi turned over and groaned. Together they helped Magnus to his feet.

Lena came up close to the torch and noticed him. "Juan!" She took his embedded face in her hands and he opened his eyes completely. "Are you all right, Juan?"

"It burns," Obrion said.

Gradually the tingling was turning cold, an ancient cold born of a pitiable malfunction that had returned to plague them again, one that would not have occurred once in a thousand years—but time had generously provided more than enough millenia to help it happen, and more than once. It had nearly killed his friends, threatening Magnus once before, and would claim him shortly if he was not freed.

"Juan," Lena said, "there's no way we can pull you free. Your hands and shoulders are not visible. We can't get a hold!"

"The portal is just barely glowing," Malachi said. He walked up to it several times but the dissolve would not activate.

"Try and push your hands through!" Lena shouted.

Juan pushed again. *We've been given a round trip by this mighty technology,* he thought, *bridging countless light years of darkness to arrive at a trap. Even the mightiest things have a right to fail. No, it wasn't failing. It's taking me as payment . . .*

He hated the superstition rising up inside him as he strained. "Lena," he managed to say, "see if the packs are coming through, even a little."

"Yes, they are, Juan, I can see them!"

Immediately Malachi and Rassmussen came up and grabbed a part of each pack. Slowly they pulled as Obrion pushed. "Lena," he shouted, "put your arms around Mal's waist and pull . . ."

When she was in position, they all pulled and Juan pushed. Slowly he began to feel that his shoulders were moving, even as a cold death continued to steal into his bones, despite the heavy clothing. He opened his mouth and took in great gulps of air.

"Quick, grab his hands!" Malachi shouted.

The two men grabbed his now exposed wrists. Their fingers felt hot on his skin. For a moment he thought that they would break off his frozen hands, leaving his cold blood to flow sluggishly from twin spouts.

"Pull!" Magnus grunted and they jerked him through as if removing a fly from ointment. Obrion went down in a heap of bodies, backpacks and the wildly stabbing beam of the torch. Suddenly he felt the blood resuming its motion through his body, and he lost consciousness as it flooded his brain.

RASSMUSSEN WAS SAYING, "Once we get above the control pit in this ship, we'll continue toward the lock at the end of the winding passage. Everything seems to be the same. When we go through the lock, we'll know if we're still on the other ship, or on earth, once and for all."

"We cannot go back," Lena said, "wherever we are."

Obrion sat up slowly. Only one of the torches was on, pointed upward.

"How do you feel?" Lena asked.

"I'll be all right." He got to his feet and stood up as straight as he could in the darkness, remembering the pride in his father's voice when he had told him to stand straight as a boy. "Let's get going."

"Juan," Lena said, touching his arm, "thanks for getting us through the door, from all of us."

"Where's my torch?" he asked.

She handed it to him.

"Mal and I will carry the packs," Rassmussen said.

Obrion turned on the torch and cast the beam ahead into the dark corridor. He led the way, putting one foot in front of the other like a condemned man who does not believe in the reprieve just given him. He quickened his pace, feeling that he had just come fully awake, dismissing the continuing sense of doom hovering at the edges of his mind.

He was silent, not once looking back through all the kilometers of winding climb which led up the constant slope to the inner door of the ship's lock.

OBRION WALKED ACROSS the last few feet of black floor toward the lock. It glowed open as he came through, and he was grateful for its smooth operation.

The others came through behind him and stood by his side, looking at the place where the outer lock would be.

Lena clicked on her torch. "Looks normal enough to me," she said. "But you know, maybe the gravitational sensation in here has nothing to do with where we are. The ship does generate its own, and might have been set at an earth-like force for comfort, one not *quite* matching what we experienced on the other ship. We could be on the moon."

"But there's the magnetic north," Malachi said.

"That could be explained in other ways," Obrion said.

"You're right," Rassmussen said.

"The rest of you go back inside the ship," Obrion said. "I'll open the outer lock. If there's no air, I'll try to back up quickly so it will close."

They did not turn to leave him.

"There's no point in all of us getting hurt," he said, "don't worry, I'll have plenty of time to get back inside the inner door."

Lena came up to him and shone the light near his face. Juan knew that he was sweating, and he felt the set expression in his face.

"One of us has to do this, Lena," he said.

Silently she let the light fall from his face, and turned to the others.

"Let me do it," Malachi said, "you've done enough, old man."

"It's my responsibility—get going."

Juan watched as one by one they went through the opening of the doorway back into the dark ship. *How long have the lights been off in this vessel*, he wondered as it glowed shut. Then he turned and stepped in front of the outer lock. The circle opened to show him a wall of earth pressing in. A clod of dirt detached itself and fell in, breaking apart at his feet. *The ship is buried, and us with it. But how far down? And where?*

As he turned away, the outer lock closed, pushing in some more loose earth.

16. The Way Out

Obrion tripped the inner lock door and told them to come inside.

"We're buried," he said. "Take off your packs and let's get out the collapsible spades so we can start digging out."

Lena put both torches in the middle of the floor as Malachi and Rassmussen took out the pieces and assembled them into four two foot spades. Obrion and Malachi started digging, alternating with Rassmussen and Lena in half hour shifts. After two hours they were all exhausted and the result was a shallow tunnel running only five feet past the open lock into the rocky earth.

"There's food in the packs," Lena said, "maybe we should rest."

"We might need those supplies if we have to trek anywhere," Obrion said.

"The ships are the same from what I can see," Lena said, "so there should be a cafeteria down the passage. We can make more before we leave."

"Should we risk it?" Magnus asked. "We might have more problems with the dissolving doorways—our luck will run out."

"Juan, we're almost home," Lena said.

"Are we? Even if we're on earth we might be a thousand miles from nowhere."

"We have to dig out," Malachi said. "I'm for checking over the café so we can save the food in the packs. Then let's get back to digging."

Juan tried to smile. "Okay, let's get down there."

AT THE ENTRANCE, Magnus shone his torch at the portal. He stepped close and it glowed dull red.

"It seems okay," Malachi said from the darkness.

"Maybe we should throw something through," Lena said.

Juan watched as Magnus took a ring from his finger and tossed it into the portal. The doorway glowed and the ring was gone.

"Of course it might be stuck and we'd never know it," Obrion said.

Magnus went through suddenly—

—and was back in less than ten seconds.

"Ah, despair!" Malachi said. "It makes one hungry." He picked up the one pack they had brought with them from the lock and went through the portal. Lena followed immediately.

"Coming?" Magnus asked and gave him the torch before going inside.

Juan came up to the portal and trembled with the memory of fear. But he mastered the feeling and stepped forward—

—into a lighted chamber which looked exactly like the other one.

"The lights are on here," Malachi said, "must be another fuse line."

AS THEY ATE their self-heating packets of duplicated fish protein and vegetables, Rassmussen said, "The dissolving doors are a *perfect* safety feature. Each chamber is perfectly sealed until the protean moment when someone goes through, and each chamber has its own life support—light, heat and duplicated air. I think the duplicator makes everything from raw materials. Now the locks and the winding passage are something else. The locks open and can stay open so you can *see* through them. But the entire corkscrew corridor can become a perfect vacuum and the chambers will stay filled with life support. There's no way one of the dissolvers can open and *stay* . . ."

Juan thought of the recliners in the pit below. Somehow the thought of seeking out that room in this ship seemed strange. The vessel seemed less friendly, more cold, but that was perhaps because he knew it was more damaged. He looked up from his empty packet of food. "Shall we get some sleep, or go back to digging?"

"I won't be able to sleep," Lena said, "until we know."

"I'm for pushing on," Malachi said.

"I can always unroll a pack and lie down in the lock while we're digging," Rassmussen said, "but I don't think I can sleep either. Let's get back to the digging right now."

AFTER AN HOUR of digging straight up at the end of their five foot tunnel, Juan's spade went through into an open space.

"I've broken through!" Quickly he started to widen the hole. Perhaps he had only found a space of some kind in the ground above the ship and was still far short of their goal.

"Malachi, come up below me quick!" Obrion shouted.

In a moment Obrion was on Malachi's shoulders and pushing dirt upward through the widening hole. Finally he put his hands up and pulled himself through for a look—and saw Luna riding high above a dark land that breathed with a hot humid wind, the familiar moon of ages, shield for lovers, puller of tides, and the place from which humankind planned to look outward to the stars, preparing for the day when a first, frail vessel would creep across the solar system bound for Alpha Centauri, a round trip of a scant twenty years. Once such a dream would have seemed grand to him. But as he noticed the dawn's light behind what looked like a jungle, he knew that he had seen realities greater than current dreams, and still larger dreams in which lay new responsibilities for himself and all who lived on earth.

"We're home!" he shouted downward. "I can see the moon, a full moon, and it's ours!"

"What luck we missed an overcast," Malachi mumbled from below.

"Let me down," Obrion said loudly.

THEY CAME OUT of the ground with the dawn, and saw that the ship was entombed within a large mound-like hill. Around it lay jungle, a thick carpet of trees, brush, and vines. The sun was just up over the trees on the horizon, a ball of white-hot iron dripping light. Moisture was coming up from the rain forest, the reverse rain of the water cycle.

"Looks like the Amazon," Malachi said, "but very much home with old sol's smashing heat."

Obrion walked to the top of the round hill and looked around. *We can still die here,* he thought. *No one knows where we are, we don't know where we are, and we have no radio. We can't walk through all that without a trail or a guide.*

Lena came up and stood next to him holding his arm. "You're still worried. But we've come this far, and we can last a little longer." He was quiet. "I'm trying to cheer you up."

"Maybe if I stay cheerless, it might improve our chances. It's a feeling that stays with me, a feeling that to be realistic one must cultivate pessimism."

Malachi and Rassmussen joined them on the hilltop. "We'd better get rid of our outer clothing," the Kenyan said.

One by one they took off their heavy parkas and double overpants, until they were each wearing only a shirt and slacks and boots. "The green matches the jungle," Malachi said.

"I have flares in the pack," Obrion said.

They brought up the two remaining packs and threw their heavy clothes down into the hole.

"Listen, you hear that noise?" Obrion asked.

"Sounds like machines," Lena said. She pointed toward the hot sun. "It's coming from there."

They all stood up and listened. "There must be people nearby," Lena said.

"Let's cover up the hole," Obrion said, "so no one finds it."

Lena and Rassmussen brought branches and a few rocks from the hillside. Obrion used them and the dug-up dirt to cover their exit.

"It'll grow over soon," Magnus said.

Quickly, Obrion and Malachi put on the two packs

and led the way down to the jungle, heading east, in the direction of the sounds.

"I feel naked without the heavy clothing," Juan said.

"We'll be bathing in humidity soon," Malachi said, "so fear not."

They came to the jungle almost immediately, and trying to enter it was worse than tunneling through a stone wall. Lacking a machete, Juan tried to hack out a trail ahead of them with his spade. Malachi worked next to him, with disappointing results.

"It'll take hours to go a few hundred feet," Lena said, looking at their accomplishment.

"What choice do we have?" Rassmussen asked. Obrion saw that already all their shirts were stained with sweat.

Inexorably, the sun rose high enough to beat down on them between the trees, its shafts like hot laser beams controlled by the fluttering filter of green leaves.

Juan continued to beat his way forward through the vines and underbrush, grateful that they at least had heavy boots and pants coarse enough to protect them from insects and snake bites. Next to him Malachi had fallen into a rhythm of tireless work.

"You've done this . . . before," Juan said between breaths.

"Of course. I'm very valuable, master."

"The sound, it's getting louder," Lena said from behind.

Juan knew that they would have to reach help by early afternoon, otherwise they would not have the strength to go back along their trail to the ship. He did not want to spend the night in the jungle. They would have to break through to the sound, and hope it was a sound made by people who could help them.

JUST BEFORE NOON the jungle fell away in front of them, suddenly revealing a roadway under construction below. Obrion led them to the edge, where they stopped. Below, all the heavy machinery was at a standstill, and no one was to be seen anywhere.

The sound returned abruptly, a dull machine-gun-like patter. A man darted out from behind a bulldozer and ran up the road, spraying the jungle to his left with an automatic weapon. Ten other men appeared like rats from behind trailers parked on the other side of the unfinished road. They all wore fibrous body armor and face masks, as well as helmets. They fired into the jungle on both sides as they ran. There was a reply of arrows, spears and the whistle of darts.

Then it was quiet again. Obrion shouted to the men below, who stood like statues on the road, each staring upward into a different section of forest. "Don't shoot, we're friends!" They turned to look up at him, pointing their weapons. Juan stood up with his hands raised, knowing that the word *friend* here meant only that foreign intruders stick together.

Someone shouted at him in Portuguese.

"He wants us to come down," Obrion said, starting to lead the way.

When they emerged on a portion of paved road, the armed figures immediately encircled them.

The one who seemed to be the leader came up to Obrion, lifted his face mask and demanded to know who they all were.

"Do you speak English?"

"Yes, I do," the big man said. "Who are you!"

"We're a UN scientific team," Juan said. "We're not armed."

"Are there more?"

"No." Juan noticed that the group seemed to stiffen at the mention of the UN.

"Are you inspectors?" the big man asked.

Juan suddenly understood. These were contractors who were illegally building a road through the jungle, moving natives out of the way, fighting the lush growth which would destroy their road in a year. But not before the road had given them what they wanted. Then the natives would come back like the green vegetation, their numbers greatly reduced. Over the years such road workers had become mercenaries, serving the wildcat companies that continued to plunder much of South America. Too often the UN was late in the enforcement of its protection laws. Observers had reported wholesale murder, the swindling of natives, airdrops of contaminated food, anything that would get a tribe out of a desirable area. This had gone on for most of a century.

"We're just lost," Juan said, knowing that the other was considering whether he should kill them on the spot. "Can you radio for help?"

All at once the big man smiled, having decided what course to take. "Of course," he said. "There is a government airfield nearby, and we have a helicopter link with it. A plane leaves for Lima twice a week. Or you could wait for the plane for Brasilia in five days." He held up five fingers. "Fortunate for us all the natives do not have guns, so they cannot damage the road, only human flesh." He looked at the gun in his hand and smiled. "No bullets, just trank pellets. Better this way than their way." He looked at each of them as he said the words, but the undercurrent of fear and the tacit sense of wrong was plain. "This way—please," the big man said, holding his non-lethal weapon in one hand and pointing toward the largest trailer with the other.

"Thank you," Obrion said and motioned for the others to follow. He looked back at the faceless men who had lowered their weapons to point at the pavement.

"We must build Brazil," the big man said.

IN THE TRANSPORT HELICOPTER Lena sat with her back to the window and asked Juan, "Are we what's left of the starcrossers?"

Obrion looked at her from across the narrow aisle where he sat between Malachi and Rassmussen. For a moment he wondered how much of the starfolk might be present in Lena's gaze as she asked the question. "I doubt it very much," he answered finally. "Too much history points the other way, that we're original to the earth."

"It may flatter some to think so," Magnus said, "and thirty years ago some such theories had a great vogue, and were believed on the basis of no evidence at all, except wish-fulfillment. The notion assumes that the human species could not have made it from scratch on its own, so help came from the stars. I think we did make it on our own—if we can take pride in where we are, even if elsewhere others progressed further. Even if they did visit us at some time in the past. It's a long way from these things to tracing lineage."

"We're still our jolly old selves," Malachi said, "even those chaps laying the bit of road with blood for water in their cement. They probably up the dosage in their tranquilizer pellets, just for fun. That's us, whoever we are."

They were silent as the copter neared the field.

AN OLD LEARJET took them off a dirt runway into a cloudless blue sky, which turned cloudy as they passed over the Andes.

"I'm still not clear on what killed the starcrossers when they visited earth," Lena said as they sat in a green carpeted lounge in two pairs of facing seats.

"I don't think we'll know the exact details for a long time," Rassmussen said next to her.

"The ships may still pose a danger to us," Malachi said.

Juan was looking out the window at the crumpled furrows of earth which were the mountains.

"Incidentally," Malachi continued next to him, "are we the same people who stepped into the subspace transmat, or are we exact duplicates of the four who perished out there?"

"We're the same," Rassmussen said, *"only* if the same atoms were transmitted through the links, the same atoms which stepped into the transmat frames we used. But if only the *pattern* of ourselves was sent and made over from raw energy at the receiving end, then we're only the twins of our originals who no longer exist. We'll never feel this, or really know which is the case until we know more about the starcrosser technology, but we are well . . . we are ourselves, and they're gone, whoever they were."

"But we are exactly like *them,* if such is the case," Malachi said, "with the same memories—then what is the difference that distinguishes?"

"You've said it yourself," Rassmussen countered. "We're like *them, another set,* twins, if the same atoms were not sent."

Juan stole a glance at Lena, then continued looking out at the mountains, wondering what other traces the starcrossers might have left on earth, still hidden. *We can't have humanity swarming through the deserted systems of the starfolk, not if we can still behave like barbarians. A deserted web and the worlds it links would be staked out into territories to be defended by local whims and force of arms . . .* Suddenly he was afraid that the roadbuilders would find the starship and deliver it into private hands. But his fear subsided as he realized that they would not dig up a mountainside for no reason. And roads were not best built over hills.

"Why do you suppose," Malachi was asking, "these star traveling fellows failed to stick around for use of their web and its transmat improvement?"

"We can only guess," Rassmussen answered. "A huge web like that could conceivably gobble up the energy output of whole galaxies, draining suns of life too quickly."

"Why should that bother them?" Malachi asked. "There are nations on earth who use most of the planet's resources. And they'll be using most of what the solar system has to offer after the turn of the century."

"Maybe the starcrossers came to believe that what they were doing was wrong?" Lena said.

"But where did they *go?*" Malachi asked.

Rassmussen shrugged. "It may be fair to say that something happened to change things for them completely. Maybe they left the expanding clump of matter that is our universe, to find other universes in superspace, that open realm in which our universe swims. Maybe they became beings without physical instrumentality. Or perhaps they died of something too subtle for them to understand. Or worst of all, maybe they've expanded operations on some vast scale in which our universe is only one unit . . ."

"I don't believe they could have become such infinite scoundrels," Lena said.

"We're responsible for what we found," Obrion said, bringing them back to the one topic they all feared. "We should be thinking about whether we want the kind of people we know to handle it. You can bet Summet and Dimitryk will be at the airport to greet us. They both know enough to want to deny us our freedom for the rest of our lives."

They were all silent. Juan watched as the jet whispered into sight of the Pacific ocean. *We've come back across time,* he thought, *from the dying edge of the universe where galaxies are fleeing ever faster into the mad dark—we've come back to a younger time of lighted spaces and unbegun beginnings. Maybe the starcrossers had simply grown weary of venturings and had decided to die? And their ships were perhaps slightly used toys thrown away for lesser beings to find. What beckoning beyond had they followed?*

Juan closed his eyes and saw the ship in the hill, surrounded by jungle. And he realized that strangeness is only the ordinary come from afar to a lesser time and place. Ignorance supports the sense of wonder and the reality of the unusual; while knowledge dispels magic and the miraculous, begetting in their place the sense of the ordinary, and all the responsibilities born from dreams. He felt the presence of the starship in the jungle, and its twin left so far away in a strange port. He thought of the sun, wondering if the starcrossers had placed a station in its other-space . . .

Looking out the window, he saw the vast Pacific, seemingly different after all the light years, yet still the same as when Balboa had first sighted it. *How much of the others did we invent,* Juan asked himself, *in our clumsy efforts to understand? How much that was left of them understood us?*

As he looked out at the earth, then at Lena, Malachi and Rassmussen, he was certain that home could never be the same again for any of them.

No. 13 **Blake's Progress** by R. F. Nelson
An 18th Century time-traveler sweeps into the future dragging his terrified wife along.

No. 14 **Birthright** by Kathleen Sky
In a world where android means slave, Andros discovers he may not be human, but one of *Them*.

No. 15 **The Star Web** by George Zebrowski
A research team uncovers an ancient civilization that sweeps from the Antarctic to the stars.

No. 16 **Kane's Odyssey** by Jeff Clinton
Seeking freedom in the city, Kane is accused of a past life he never knew he'd lived.

No. 17 **The Black Roads** by Joseph Hensley
Kill or be killed, in a future America where life is lived totally on the roads.

No. 18 **Legacy** by J. F. Bone
Tonocaine is a drug that drives men mad. Williams has to find who's inflicting it on the universe.

USE THIS HANDY FORM TO ORDER YOUR BOOKS